WE LOVE
GLENDA
SO MUCH
AND OTHER
TALES

Translated from
the Spanish by
Gregory Rabassa

Alfred A. Knopf
New York 1983

WE LOVE GLENDA SO MUCH

AND OTHER TALES

JULIO CORTÁZAR

THIS IS A BORZOI BOOK
PUBLISHED BY ALFRED A. KNOPF, INC.

Library of Congress Cataloging in Publication Data
Cortázar, Julio.
We love Glenda so much, and other tales.
Translation of: Queremos tanto a Glenda.
Contents: Orientation of cats—We love Glenda so
much—Story with spiders—[etc.]
I. Title.
PQ7797.C7145Q413   1983   863   82-48718
ISBN 0-394-52493-4

Manufactured in the United States of America
Published March 29, 1983
Second Printing Before Publication

CONTENTS

ORIENTATION
OF CATS

To Juan Soriano

When Alana and Osiris look at me I can't complain of the least dissembling, the least duplicity. They look at me straight on, Alana with her blue light and Osiris with his green ray. They also look at one another that way, Alana stroking Osiris's black back as he lifts his mouth from the plate of milk and mews with satisfaction, woman and cat knowing one another on planes that escape me, that my caresses can't reach. For some time now I've renounced all mastery over Osiris, we're good friends across an unbridgeable distance; but Alana is my wife and the distance between us is a different one, something that she doesn't seem to feel but which blocks my happiness when Alana looks at me, when she looks at me straight on just the way Osiris does and smiles at me or speaks to me without the slightest reserve, giving herself in every gesture and everything, just as she gives herself in love, there where her whole body is like her eyes: an absolute surrender, an uninterrupted reciprocity.

It's strange—even though I've renounced entry into Osiris's world, my love for Alana won't accept that simplicity of a thing concluded, of partners forever, of life without secrets. Behind those blue eyes there's more, in the depths of the words and moans and the silences another realm is born, another Alana is breathing. I've never told her so, I love her too much to break this surface of happiness over which so many days have slipped, so many years. In my own way I make a stubborn effort to understand, to discover; I watch her but without spying; I follow her but without mistrust; I love a marvelous mutilated statue, an unfinished text, a fragment of sky inscribed on the window of life.

There was a time when music seemed to me to be the path that would really lead me to Alana; watching her listen to our Bartók, Duke Ellington, and Gal Costa records, a gradual transparency sank me into her, the music undressed her in a different way, turned her more and more Alana, because Alana couldn't be only that woman who had always looked at me straight on without hiding anything from me. Against Alana, beyond Alana, I was looking for her in order to love her better; and if at first the music let me glimpse other Alanas, the day came when facing a Rembrandt print I saw her change even more, as if a set of clouds in the sky had suddenly altered the lights and shadows of a landscape. I felt that the painting was carrying her beyond herself for that only spectator who could measure the instantaneous metamorphosis that was never repeated, the glimpse of Alana in Alana. Involuntary interceders, Keith Jarrett, Beethoven, and Aníbal Troilo had helped me get close, but facing a painting or a print Alana got rid of even more of what she thought she was. For a moment she would enter an imaginary world so that without knowing it she could get out of herself, going from one painting to another, making comments on them or being silent, a deck of cards that each new contemplation shuffled for the one who, stealthy and attentive, a little behind or leading her by the arm, saw coming one after another the queens and the aces, the spades and the clubs— Alana.

What could be done with Osiris? Give him his milk, leave him alone as a satisfied and purring black ball; but Alana I could take to this picture gallery as I did yesterday, go to a theater with mirrors and camera obscuras once more, with sharp images on the canvas facing that other image, gay in blue jeans and a red blouse, who after putting out her cigarette at the entrance would go from picture to picture, stopping at precisely the distance her look required, turning to me from time to time to comment or compare. She had never discovered that I wasn't there for the pictures, that a little to the rear or to the side my way of looking had nothing to do with hers. She probably never realized that her slow and reflective pace from picture to picture was changing her until I had to close my eyes and struggle against squeezing her in my arms and going off into a delirium with her, into a full-fledged bit of madness right out in public. Relaxed, light in her natural way of pleasure and discovery, her pauses and her lingering were inscribed in a different time from mine, alien to the tense expectancy of my thirst.

Until then everything had been a vague omen, Alana in the music, Alana facing Rembrandt. But now my hope was beginning to be unbearably fulfilled; from the moment of our arrival Alana had given herself over to the paintings with the atrocious innocence of a chameleon, going from one state to another without knowing that a spectator in ambush was spying on her posture, the tilt of her head, the movement of her hands or her lips, seeking the inner chromatism that ran through her until it showed her to be another, there where the other one was always Alana adding herself to Alana, the cards piling up until the deck is complete. By her side, going slowly along the walls of the gallery, I was watching her give herself over to each painting, my eyes were multiplying the lightning bolt of a triangle that went from her to the picture and from the picture to me, returning to her and catching the change, the different halo that encircled her for a moment to give way later to a new aura, a tonality that exposed her to the true one, to the ultimate nakedness. It was impossible to foresee how far that osmosis would be repeated, how many new Alanas would finally carry me to the synthesis from which we would both emerge fulfilled, she without knowing it and lighting a new cigarette before asking me to buy her a drink; I knowing that my long search had finally culminated and that from then on my love would take in the visible and the invisible, would accept Alana's clean look without the uncertainty of closed doors, forbidden passageways.

Opposite a solitary boat and a foreground of black rocks, I watched her remain motionless for a long time; an imperceptible fluttering of her hands made her seem to be swimming in the air, going out to sea, a flight from horizons. I was no longer able to be surprised that the other painting, where a spike-topped grating cut off access to the bordering trees, made her step back as if seeking the proper focus. Suddenly it was repulsion, the rejection of an unacceptable limit. Birds, marine monsters, windows opening onto silence or letting a simulacrum of death enter—each new painting was dragging Alana along, despoiling her of her previous color, pulling the modulations of freedom out of her, of flying, of wide-open spaces, affirming her negation facing night and nothingness, her solar anxiety, her almost terrible impulse of a phoenix bird. I remained in back, knowing that it would be impossible for me to bear her look, her interrogative surprise when she saw in my face the bewilderment of confirmation, because that too was I, that was my Project Alana, my Alana life, it had been desired by me and reined in by a present tense of city and parsimony, finally now Alana, finally Alana and I from now on. I would have liked to have held her naked in my arms, love her in such a way that everything would be clear, everything would be spoken forever between us, and that from that endless night of love (as we had already known so many of them) the first dawn of life would be born.

We got to the end of the gallery; I went over to an exit door, still hiding my face, hoping that the air and the street-lights would turn me back into what Alana knew of me. I saw her stop in front of a picture that other visitors had hidden from me, remain motionless for a long time looking at the painting of a window and a cat. One last transformation made her a slow statue neatly separated from the others, from me, who went over indecisively seeking the eyes lost in the canvas. I saw that the cat was identical to Osiris and that it was looking at something in the distance that the sidewall of the window prevented us from seeing. Motionless in his contem-plation, he seemed less motionless than Alana's immobility. In some way I felt that the triangle had been broken; when Alana turned her head toward me the triangle no longer existed, she had gone into the picture but she hadn't come back, she was still beside the cat, looking beyond the window where no one could see what they saw, what only Alana and Osiris saw every time they looked at me straight on.

WE LOVE
GLENDA
SO MUCH

In those days it was hard to know. You go to the movies or the theater and live your night without thinking about the people who have already gone through the same ceremony, choosing the place and the time, getting dressed and telephoning and row eleven or five, the darkness and the music, territory that belongs to nobody and to everybody there where everybody is nobody, the men or women in their seats, maybe a word of apology for arriving late, a murmured comment that someone picks up or ignores, almost always silence, looks pouring onto the stage or the screen, fleeing from what's beside them, from what's on this side. It was really hard to know that there were so many of us—beyond the ads, the endless lines, the posters, and the reviews—so many who loved Glenda.

It took three or four years, and it would not be bold to assert that the nucleus had its start with Irazusta or Diana Rivero; they themselves didn't know how at some moment, over drinks with friends after the movies, things were said or left unsaid that suddenly would form the alliance, what afterward we all called the nucleus and the younger ones the club. There was nothing of a club about it, we simply loved Glenda Garson, and that was enough to set us apart from those who only admired her. Just like them, we admired Glenda too, and also Anouk, Marilyn, Annie, Silvana, and why not Marcello, Yves, Vittorio, or Dirk, but only we loved Glenda so much, and the nucleus was formed because of that and out of that, it was something that only we knew, and we trusted in those who all during our conversations had shown little by little that they loved Glenda too.

Starting with Diana or Irazusta, the nucleus was slowly expanding. In the year of *Snow Fire* there couldn't have been more than six or seven of us; with the premiere of *The Uses of Elegance* the nucleus broadened and we felt that it was growing at an almost unbearable rate and that we were threatened with snobbish imitation or seasonal sentimentality. The first, Irazusta and Diana and two or three more of us, decided to close ranks, not to admit anyone without a test, without an examination disguised under the whiskey and a show of erudition (so Buenos Aires, so London and Mexico, those midnight exams). At the time of the opening of *Fragile Returns*, we had to admit, melancholically triumphant, that there were many of us who loved Glenda. The chance meetings at the movies, the glances exchanged as we came out, that kind of lost look on the women and the painful silence of the men, showed us better than any insignia or password. Mechanics that defied investigation led us to the same downtown café, the isolated tables began to draw closer together, there was the gracious custom of ordering the same cocktail so as to lay aside any useless skirmishing, and finally looking each other in the eyes, there where Glenda's last image in the last scene of the last movie still breathed.

Twenty, maybe thirty, we never knew how many we had come to be, because sometimes Glenda would go on for months at one theater or was in two or three at the same time, and there was also that exceptional moment when she appeared onstage to play the young murderess in *The Lunatics* and her success broke the dikes and created a momentary enthusiasm that we never accepted. By that time we already knew each other; a lot of us would visit each other to talk about Glenda. From the very beginning Irazusta seemed to exercise a tacit command that he had never asked for, and Diana Rivero played her slow chess game of acceptance and rejection that assured us a total authenticity without the risk of infiltrators or boobs. What had begun as a free association was now attaining the structure of a clan, and the casual interrogations of early times had been succeeded by concrete questions, the stumbling scene in *The Uses of Elegance*, the final retort in *Snow Fire*, the second erotic scene in *Fragile Returns*. We loved Glenda so much that we couldn't tolerate parvenus, rowdy lesbians, erudite aestheticians. It was even (we'll never know how) taken for granted that we would go to the café on Fridays when a Glenda movie was playing downtown, and with the reruns in neighborhood theaters we would let a week go by before getting together in order to give everybody the necessary time; like a rigorous regulation, the obligations were defined without error; not respecting them would have meant provoking Irazusta's contemptuous smile or that graciously horrible look with which Diana Rivero denounced and punished treason.

At that time the gatherings were only Glenda, her dazzling presence in every one of us, and we knew nothing of discrepancies or misgivings. Only gradually, at first with a feeling of guilt, did some dare to let partial criticisms slip, disillusion or disappointment with an unfortunate scene, descents into the conventional or the predictable. We knew that Glenda wasn't responsible for the weaknesses that at certain moments clouded the splendid crystal of *The Lash* or the ending of *You Never Know Why*. We found out about other films by the directors, where the stories and the scripts came from, we were implacable with them because we were beginning to feel that our love for Glenda was going beyond the merely artistic terrain and that she alone was saved from what the rest did imperfectly. Diana was the first to talk about a mission; she did it in her tangential way, not stating outright what really counted for her. We saw the joy of a double whiskey, of a satisfied smile in her when we admitted openly that it was true, that we couldn't just stay like that, the movies and the café and loving Glenda so much.

Not even then were clear words spoken; we didn't need them. All that counted was Glenda's happiness in each one of us, and that happiness could only come from perfection. Suddenly the mistakes, the misses, became unbearable for us; we couldn't accept the way *You Never Know Why* ended, or that *Snow Fire* should include the infamous poker scene (in which Glenda didn't take part, but which in some way stained her like vomit—that expression of Nancy Phillips's) and the inadmissible arrival of the repentant son. As almost always, it was up to Irazusta to give a clear definition of the mission that awaited us, and that night we went home as if crushed by the responsibility we had just recognized and assumed, catching a glimpse at the same time of the happiness of a flawless future, of Glenda without blunders or betrayals.

Instinctively, the nucleus closed ranks, the task wouldn't allow for a hazy plurality. Irazusta spoke of the laboratory after it had already been set up in a country house in Recife de Lobos. We divided up the tasks equitably among those who were to collect all the prints of *Fragile Returns,* chosen for its relatively few imperfections. No one had thought to raise the question of money; Irazusta had been Howard Hughes's partner in the Pichincha tin mines, an extremely simple mechanism put the necessary power in our hands, jets and connections and bribes. We didn't even have an office; Hagar Loss's computer programmed the tasks and the stages. Two months after Diana Rivero's remark the laboratory was all set up to replace the ineffective bird scene in *Fragile Returns* with a different one that gave Glenda back the perfect rhythm and the exact feeling of the dramatic action. The film was already several years old and its rerun on international circuits didn't cause the slightest surprise; memory plays with its repositories and makes them accept their own permutations and variants, perhaps Glenda herself wouldn't have noticed the change but would have noticed, because we all had, the marvel of perfect coincidence with a memory washed clean of slag, precisely in tune with desire.

The mission was being accomplished without surcease; as soon as we felt sure that the laboratory was in working order we brought off the rescue of *Snow Fire* and *The Prism:* the other films entered into the process with the exact rhythm foreseen by Hagar Loss's personnel and the people in the laboratory. We had problems with *The Uses of Elegance* because people in the oil-producing emirates owned copies for their personal enjoyment and extraordinary maneuvers and procedures were necessary in order to steal them (there's no reason to use any other word) and to steal them without their owners' noticing. The laboratory was functioning at a level of perfection that had seemed unattainable to us at the start, even though we hadn't dared say so to Irazusta; curiously, the most doubtful one had been Diana; but when Irazusta showed us *You Never Know Why* and we saw the real ending, we saw Glenda, who instead of going back to Romano's house, headed her car toward the cliff and destroyed us with her splendid, necessary fall into the torrent, we knew that there could be perfection in this world and that now it belonged to Glenda, to Glenda for us forever.

The most difficult part was, of course, deciding on the changes, the cuts, the modifications in montage and rhythm; our different ways of feeling Glenda brought on harsh confrontations that calmed down only after long analyses and in some cases the imposition of majority rule in the nucleus. But while some of us, defeated, watched the new version with bitterness over the fact that it wasn't completely up to our dreams, I don't think anyone was disappointed with the finished work, we loved Glenda so much that the results were always justifiable, often beyond what had been foreseen. There were even a few scares, a letter from a reader of the inevitable *Times* of London showing surprise that three scenes in *Snow Fire* had been shown in a different order from how the writer thought he remembered, and also an article in *La Opinión* protesting a supposed cut in *The Prism*, imagining the hand of bureaucratic prudishness. In every case rapid arrangements were made in order to avoid possible follow-ups; it wasn't hard, people are fickle and forget or accept or are in search of what's new, the movie world is ephemeral, like the historical present, except for those of us who love Glenda so much.

Basically more dangerous were the arguments within

the nucleus, risking schism or diaspora. Even though we felt more united than ever because of the mission, there were nights when analytical voices contaminated by political philosophies were raised, bringing up moral problems in the midst of the work, asking if we weren't surrendering to an onanistic hall of mirrors, foolishly carving a piece of baroque madness on an ivory tusk or a grain of rice. It wasn't easy to turn our backs on them because the nucleus had only been able to do its work in the way a heart or an airplane does: by maintaining a perfectly coherent rhythm. It wasn't easy to listen to criticism that accused us of escapism, that suspected a waste of strength that was being turned away from a more pressing reality, one that was more in need of agreement in the times we were living. And yet it wasn't necessary to crush summarily a heresy that was only hinted at, as even its protagonists limited themselves to a partial objection, they and we loved Glenda so much that above and beyond ethical or historical disagreements the feeling that would always unite us remained, the certainty that perfecting Glenda was perfecting us and perfecting the world. We even had splendid recompense in the fact that one of the philosophers re-established the equilibrium after overcoming that period of inane scruples; from his mouth we heard that all partial works are also history, that something as immense as the invention of the printing press had been born of the most individual and particular of desires—to repeat and perpetuate a woman's name.

In that way we came to the day on which we got proof that Glenda's image was now being projected without the slightest weakness; the screens of the world were presenting her in just the way that she herself—we were sure—would have wanted to be presented, and perhaps that was why it didn't surprise us too much to read in the press that she had just announced her retirement from movies and the theater. Glenda's involuntary and marvelous contribution to our work couldn't have been either coincidence or miracle, it was simply that something in her had unknowingly respected our anonymous love, from the depths of her being came the only answer that she could give us, the act of love that included us in one last act of giving, the one that ordinary people would only understand as an absence. We were living the happiness of the seventh day, of the rest after the creation; now we would be able to see every one of Glenda's works without the agonizing threat of a tomorrow plagued by mistakes and blunders; now we could come together with the lightness of angels or birds, in an absolute presence that was like eternity.

Yes, but a poet had said under Glenda's same skies that eternity is in love with the works of time, and it was for Diana to discover and give us the news a year later. Ordinary and human, Glenda was announcing her return to the screen, the usual reasons, the frustration of a professional with nothing to do, a role that was made to order, an imminent filming. No one can have forgotten that night at the café, precisely after seeing *The Uses of Elegance*, which was returning to downtown theaters. It almost wasn't necessary for Irazusta to say what we were all experiencing, a bitter taste of injustice and rebellion. We loved Glenda so much that our discouragement didn't touch her, it was no fault of hers, being an actress and being Glenda, the horror was in the ruptured mechanism, in the reality of figures and awards and Oscars entering our so hard-won heaven like a hidden fissure. When Diana laid her hand on Irazusta's arm and said "Yes, it's the only thing left to do," she was speaking for all of us with no need for consultation. Never had the nucleus had such a fearsome drive, never had it needed fewer words to put it into motion.

We separated, undone, already living what would happen on a day that only one of us would know ahead of time. We were sure we wouldn't meet again at the café, that each of us from then on would hide the solitary perfection of our realm. We knew that Irazusta was going to do what was necessary, nothing simpler for someone like him. We didn't even say good-bye the way we usually did, with the nice security of meeting again after the movies some night with *Fragile Returns* or *The Lash*. It was rather a turning your back, with the pretext that it was late, that you had to leave; we went off separately, each one bearing his or her desire to forget until everything was consummated, and knowing it wouldn't be that way, that we would still have to open the newspaper some morning and read the news, the stupid phrases of professional consternation. We would never talk about that with anybody, we would courteously avoid each other in theaters and on the street; it would be the only way that the nucleus could remain true to its faith, could silently guard the finished work. We loved Glenda so much that we would offer her one last inviolable perfection. On the untouchable heights to which we had raised her in exaltation, we would save her from the fall, her faithful could go on adoring her without any decrease; one does not come down from a cross alive.

STORY WITH SPIDERS

We arrived at the bungalow at two in the afternoon and half an hour later, true to the telephone appointment, the young agent appears with the keys, starts up the refrigerator, and shows us how the water heater and the air conditioner work. It's understood that we'll stay ten days, paid in advance. We open our bags and take out what we need for the beach; we'll settle in at sundown, the view of the Caribbean sparkling at the base of the hill is too tempting. We go down the sloping path, we even find a shortcut through the brush that gets us there quicker; there are only three hundred feet between the bungalows on the hill and the sea.

. . .

Last night, while we were putting our clothes away and lining up the groceries bought in Saint-Pierre, we could hear the voices of the people in the other wing of the bungalow. They speak very softly, not Martinican voices, full of color and laughter. From time to time a few clearer words: American English, tourists no doubt. The first impression is one of displeasure, we don't know why we expected complete solitude when we saw that each bungalow (there are four of them amidst flower beds, banana trees, and coconut palms) is double. Maybe because when we saw them for the first time after a complicated investigation by telephone from the Hotel de Diamant we thought that everything was vacant and at the same time strangely occupied. The open-air restaurant, for example, a hundred feet farther down: abandoned, but with a few bottles, glasses, and place settings at the bar. And in one or two of the bungalows towels, lotion or shampoo bottles, could be glimpsed in the bathrooms through the blinds. The young agent opened up a completely empty one for us, and to a vague question gave just as vague an answer: that the regular manager had gone away and he was taking charge of the bungalows because he was a friend of the owner. Better that way, of course, since we were looking for solitude and beach; but, of course, other people have thought the same thing and two female American voices are murmuring in the adjoining wing of the bungalow. Paper-thin walls, but everything so comfortable, so well set up. We slept interminably, something strange for us. And if we needed anything, that was it.

Friendships: a tame and mendicant female cat, another black one, wilder but just as hungry. The birds here almost land in your hand and the green lizards climb up onto the table in search of flies. We're surrounded by the bleating of goats far off, five cows and a calf are pastured on the highest part of the hill and they moo properly. We can also hear the dogs from the shacks at the end of the valley; the two cats will certainly join the concert tonight.

The beach deserted by European standards. A few boys are swimming and playing, black or cinnamon bodies dance on the sand. In the distance a family—countrymen or Germans, sadly white and blond—is organizing towels, suntan oils, and tote bags. We let the hours pass in the water or on the sand, incapable of anything else, prolonging the rituals of creams and cigarettes. We still haven't felt memories coming to the fore, that need to make an inventory of the past that grows with solitude and boredom. Quite the contrary: shutting out all reference to the preceding weeks, the meetings in Delft, the night at Erik's farm. If that comes back we waft it away like a puff of smoke, the slight movement of a hand that clears the air again.

Two girls go down the hillside path and pick out a distant spot, the shade of a coconut palm. We gather that they are our neighbors in the bungalow, we imagine them to be secretaries or elementary school teachers from Detroit, from Nebraska. We watch them go into the sea together, go off sportingly, return slowly, savoring the hot and transparent water, a beauty that becomes a topic only when it is described, the eternal matter of postcards. There are two sailboats on the horizon, a motorboat leaves Saint-Pierre with a woman on water skis who meritoriously gets up after every fall, and there are a lot of them.

At dusk, we've come back to the beach after a siesta, the day declines through great white clouds—we tell ourselves that this Christmas will be the perfect answer to our wishes: solitude, the assurance that no one knows where we are, being out of reach of any possible difficulties and at the same time far from the stupid gatherings that come at the end of the year and from conditioned memories, an agreeable freedom to open canned goods and mix a white rum punch made with cane sugar syrup and limes. We dine on the veranda, separated by a bamboo screen from the symmetrically placed terrace where, late now, we hear the barely murmuring voices again. We are a reciprocal marvel as neighbors, we respect each other in an almost exaggerated way. If the girls on the beach are really the occupants of the bungalow, maybe they're wondering if the two people they saw on the sand are the ones living in the other wing. Civilization does have its advantages, we recognize between drinks: no shouting, no transistors, no cheap humming. Oh, if only they'll stay here for the ten days instead of being replaced by a couple with children. Christ has been born again; for our part we can sleep.

We get up with the sun, guava juice and mugs of coffee. The night has been long, with gusts of rain confessedly tropical, quick floods that suddenly and shamedly cease. The dogs barked from every direction, although there was no moon; frogs and birds, sounds that the citified ear can't recognize but that perhaps explain the dreams that we now recall with the first cigarettes. *Aegri somnia.* Where is that from? Charles Nodier, or Nerval, sometimes we can't resist that past of libraries that other vocations have almost erased. We tell each other about dreams where larvae, uncertain threats, and unwelcome but predictable exhumations spin their webs or make us spin them. Nothing surprising after Delft (but we've decided not to bring back recent memories, there'll be time, as always. Curiously, it doesn't affect us to think about Michael, about the well on Erik's farm, things all closed up now; we almost never talk about them or about what preceded them even though we know they can be mentioned without doing us any harm. After all, pleasure and delight came from them, and the night on the farm was worth the price we're paying, but at the same time we feel all that is still too close, the details. Michael naked in the moonlight, things that we would have liked to avoid beyond the inevitable dreams; better this blocking out, then, *other voices, other rooms*: literature and airplanes, what splendid drugs).

The sea at nine in the morning carries off night's last drivel, sun and salt and sand bathe the skin with a hot touch. When we see the girls going down the path we all become aware at the same time, we look at each other. We had made only one comment, almost on the edge of sleep, late at night: at some moment the voices from the other side of the bungalow had gone from whispering to a few clearly audible phrases, even if their meaning escaped us. But it wasn't the meaning that attracted us in that exchange of words that ceased almost at once and returned to a monotone, a discreet murmur, but that one of the voices was that of a man.

At siesta time the muffled sound of conversation on the other veranda reaches us again. Without knowing why, we insist on making the two girls on the beach match the voices in the bungalow, and now that nothing makes one think of a man near them, the memory of last night is unsketched, joined to the other sounds that have aroused us, the dogs, the sudden gusts of wind and rain, the creaking on the roof. City people, people very impressionable away from their own sounds, their mannerly rainstorms.

Besides, what do we care what goes on in the bungalow

next door? The reason we're here is that we had to get away from the other thing, from other people. It's not easy to give up habits, conditioned reflexes, of course; without admitting it to ourselves, we pay attention to what's softly coming through the wall, the dialogue that we imagine to be placid and anodyne, the purring of pure routine. It's impossible to recognize words, even voices, so similar in their register that for moments one might even think it the broken parts of a monologue. That's the way they must have heard us too, but they're not listening to us, of course; to do that they'd have to be silent, they'd have to be here for reasons similar to ours, crouching vigilantly in wait like the black cat that's stalking a lizard on the veranda. But we don't interest them at all: so much the better for them. The two voices alternate, cease, start up again. And there's no man's voice, even if it were speaking that softly we would have recognized it.

As always in the tropics, night falls fast, the bungalow is poorly lighted but that doesn't bother us; we do almost no cooking, the only thing hot is the coffee. We have nothing to say to each other and maybe that's why we seek distraction in listening to the murmuring of the girls, without admitting it openly we're lying in wait for the man's voice, even though we know that no car has come up the hill and that the other bungalows are still empty. We rock in the rocking chairs and smoke in the darkness; there aren't any mosquitoes, the murmurs come from holes of silence, become still, return. If they could imagine us they wouldn't like it; it's not that we're spying on them, but they would certainly look upon us as two spiders in the darkness. After all, it doesn't upset us that the other side of the bungalow is occupied. We were looking for solitude but now we're thinking about what night would be like here if there really weren't anybody on the other side, impossible to deny that the farm, Michael, are still so close.

Having to look at each other, talk, take out the cards or the dice again. It's better like that, in the sling chairs, listening to the rather catlike murmurs until it's time to sleep.

Until it's time to sleep, but here the nights don't bring us what we'd hoped for, a no-man's-land where finally—or for a time, there's no need to pretend what's not possible— we'd be under cover of everything that begins beyond the windows. In our case too, foolishness hasn't been the strong point; we've never reached a destination without foreseeing the next one or the next ones. Sometimes it would seem that we're playing at fencing ourselves in as now on an insignificant island where anything can be easily located; but that's part of an infinitely more complex chess game in which the modest movement of a pawn conceals more important plays. The famous story of the purloined letter is objectively absurd. Objectively; the truth runs underneath, and the Puerto Ricans who for years cultivated marijuana on their New York fire escapes or smack in the middle of Central Park knew more about that than a lot of police. In any case, we're in control of immediate possibilities, ships and planes: Venezuela and Trinidad are a stone's throw away, two choices among six or seven; our passports are the kind that slip through airports with no trouble whatsoever. This innocent hill, this bungalow for petty bourgeois tourists: beautiful loaded dice that we've always known how to use at the proper moment. Delft is far, far away, Erik's farm is beginning to recede in our memories, being erased in the same way that the well and Michael fleeing in the moonlight are being erased, Michael, so white and naked in the moonlight.

. . .

The dogs howled again intermittently, from one of the shacks in the dell the shouts of a woman suddenly cut off at their highest point, the silence next door let a murmur of confused alarm pass in the dozing of tourist women too fatigued and out of it to be really interested in what surrounded them. We stayed listening, far removed from sleep. After all, what's the use of sleeping if later on it could be the roar of a cloudburst on the roof or the shrill lovemaking of cats, the preludes to nightmares, dawn, when heads finally flatten pillows and then nothing can get into them until the sun climbs up the palm trees and you have to go back to living.

On the beach, after taking a long swim out to sea, we wondered again about the abandonment of the bungalows. The restaurant hut with its glasses and bottles brings out the memory of the mystery of the *Mary Celeste* (so well known and so well read about, but that obsessive recurrence of the unexplained, the sailors boarding the ship drifting along at full sail and with nobody on board, the ashes still warm in the cook stoves, the cabins with no signs of mutiny or plague. A collective suicide? We looked at each other ironically, it's not an idea that can open a path in our way of seeing things. We wouldn't be here if we'd accepted it at one time).

The girls go down to the beach late, they sun themselves for a long time before swimming. There too, we notice without commenting, they talk to each other in low voices, and if we'd been closer we would have been reached by the same confidential murmur, the polite fear of intruding in the life of others. If at some moment they would come over to ask for a light, to find out the time . . . But the bamboo screen seems to have been extended down to the beach, we know that they won't bother us.

Siesta time is long, we don't feel like going back to the

beach nor do they, we can hear them talking in the room and then on the veranda. Alone, of course. But why of course? Night can be different and we wait for it without saying so, busying ourselves with nothing, lingering in rocking chairs and with cigarettes and drinks, leaving only one light burning on the veranda; the blinds of the living room filter it through in thin strips that don't drive off the shadows of the air, the silence of waiting. We're not waiting for anything, of course. Why of course? Why lie to ourselves if the only thing we're doing is waiting, as in Delft, as in so many other places? A person can wait for nothing or for a murmur from the other side of the thin wall, a change in the voices. Later a creaking of a bed will be heard, the silence will begin full of dogs, of foliage moved by the gusts of wind. It's not going to rain tonight.

They're leaving; at eight o'clock in the morning a taxi comes to pick them up, the black chauffeur laughs and jokes, taking out their suitcases, their beach bags, large straw hats, tennis rackets. From the veranda you can see the path, the white taxi; they can't make us out among the plants, nor do they even look in our direction.

The beach is peopled with fishermen's children who play ball before swimming, but today it seems even more empty to us now that they won't be back to swim. On the way back we take a roundabout path without realizing it, in any case, without expressly deciding upon it, and we pass in front of the other wing of the bungalow which we had always avoided. Now everything is really abandoned except for our wing. We try the door, it opens noiselessly, the girls have left the key on the inside, no doubt by agreement with the agent who will or will not come by later to clean the bungalow. It no longer surprises us that things are exposed to the whims of anyone, like the glasses and the plates from the restaurant; we see wrinkled sheets, damp towels, empty bottles, insecticides, Coca-Cola bottles and glasses, magazines in English, bars of soap. Everything is so alone, so left behind. They slept there, in the big bed with sheets with yellow flowers. The two of them. And they talked, they talked before going to sleep. They talked so much before sleeping.

The siesta hangs heavy, interminable because we don't feel like going to the beach until the sun is lower in the sky. While making coffee or washing the dishes we catch ourselves in the same position of listening, our ears intent on the wall. We should have laughed but we didn't. Not now, now that finally and really we have the solitude so sought after and so necessary, now we don't laugh.

Preparing dinner takes time, we deliberately complicate the simplest things so that everything will last and night will close in over the hill before we've finished eating. From time to time we catch ourselves looking toward the wall again, waiting for what is already so far away, a murmur that is probably continuing on an airplane or in the cabin of a ship. The agent hasn't come, we know that the bungalow is vacant and open, that it still smells of cologne and youthful skin. It suddenly gets warmer, the silence accentuates it or digestion or boredom because we sit without moving out of the rocking chairs, just barely swaying in the darkness, smoking and waiting. We won't admit it, of course, but we know that we're waiting. The sounds of the night slowly grow, faithful to the rhythm of things and stars; as if the same birds and the same frogs from last night had taken up position and begun their song at the same moment. The chorus of dogs too (*a horizon of dogs*, impossible not to recall the poem), and in the underbrush the lovemaking of the cats tears the air. All that's missing is the murmur of the two voices in the bungalow next door, and that really is silence, silence itself. Everything else slips through the ears that are absurdly concentrated on the wall as if expecting. We don't even talk, fearing that we'll crush the impossible murmurs with our voices. It's already quite late but we don't feel sleepy, the heat keeps on rising in the living room but it doesn't occur to us to open the two doors. We don't do anything but smoke and hope for the hopeless; it doesn't even occur to us, as in the beginning, that the girls might imagine us as spiders lying in wait; they're no longer there for us to attribute our own imaginations to, to turn them into mirrors of this thing taking place in the darkness, of this that unbearably isn't taking place.

Because we can't lie to ourselves, each creak of the rocking chairs replaces a dialogue but at the same time keeps it alive. Now we know that everything was useless, the running away, the trip, the hope of still finding a dark hollow without witnesses, a favorable refuge for beginning again (because repentance doesn't enter our nature, what we did is done and we'll start all over again as soon as we know we're safe from reprisals). It's as if suddenly the whole veteranship of the past has ceased to operate, has abandoned us the way the gods abandon Antony in Cavafy's poem. If we still think about the strategy that guaranteed our arrival on the island, if we imagine for a moment the possible timetables, the efficient telephones in other ports and cities, we do it with the same abstract indifference with which we so frequently quote poems while playing the infinite caroms of mental association. The worst part is that, we don't know why, the change has taken place since our arrival, since the first murmurs from the other side of the wall that we considered a mere barrier, also abstract, for solitude and rest. That another unexpected voice should be joined to the whispers was no reason to go beyond a banal summer enigma, the mystery of the room next door like that of the *Mary Celeste*, frivolous food for siestas and strolls. Nor did we give it any special importance, we've never mentioned it; we only know that it's now impossible to cease paying attention, to cease orienting all activity, all relaxation, toward the wall.

Maybe that's why late at night while we pretend to sleep, we're not disconcerted too much by the short, dry cough that comes from the other side of the bungalow, its tone unmistakably masculine. It almost isn't a cough, rather an involuntary signal, at the same time discreet and penetrating as the girls' murmurs were, but now it's a signal, now it's a summons, after so much alien chatter. We get up without speaking, silence has fallen over the living room again, only one dog is baying and baying far away. We wait for a length of time that's impossible to measure; the visitor in the bungalow is silent too, maybe he's also waiting or has gone to sleep among the yellow flowers on the sheets. It doesn't matter, now there's an agreement that has nothing to do with will, there's an ending that has no need for form or formulas; at some moment we come closer together without consulting each other, without even trying to look at each other, we know that we're thinking about Michael, about how Michael too went back to Erik's farm, went back with no apparent reason, even though the farmhouse for him was as empty as the wing of the bungalow next door, came back just as the girls' visitor has come back, just like Michael and the others, coming back like flies, coming back without knowing that they're expected, that this time they're coming to a different appointment.

At bedtime we'd put on our nightshirts as usual; now we let them drop like white, gelatinous splotches onto the floor, naked, we go toward the door and out into the garden. It's simply a matter of going around the hedge that extends the separation of the two wings of the bungalow; the door is still closed but we know that it isn't locked, that all we have to do is lift the latch. There's no light inside when we go in together; it's the first time in a long while that we lean on each other in order to walk.

II

GRAFFITI

To Antoni Tàpies

So many things begin and perhaps end as a game, I suppose
that it amused you to find the sketch beside yours, you at-
tributed it to chance or a whim and only the second time did
you realize that it was intentional and then you looked at it
slowly, you even came back later to look at it again, taking
the usual precautions: the street at its most solitary moment,
no patrol wagon on neighboring corners, approaching with
indifference and never looking at the graffiti face-on but from
the other sidewalk or diagonally, feigning interest in the shop
window alongside, going away immediately.

Your own game had begun out of boredom, it wasn't
really a protest against the state of things in the city, the
curfew, the menacing prohibition against putting up posters

or writing on walls. It simply amused you to make sketches
with colored chalk (you didn't like the term graffiti, so art
critic–like) and from time to time to come and look at them
and even, with a little luck, to be a spectator to the arrival of
the municipal truck and the useless insults of the workers as
they erased the sketches. It didn't matter to them that they
weren't political sketches, the prohibition covered everything,
and if some child had dared draw a house or a dog it would
have been erased in just the same way in the midst of curses
and threats. In the city people no longer knew too well which
side fear was really on; maybe that's why you overcame yours
and every so often picked the time and place just right for
making a sketch.

You never ran any risk because you knew how to choose
well, and in the time that passed until the cleaning trucks
arrived something opened up for you like a very clean space
where there was almost room for hope. Looking at your
sketch from a distance you could see people casting a glance
at it as they passed, no one stopped, of course, but no one
failed to look at the sketch, sometimes a quick abstract com-
position in two colors, the profile of a bird or two entwined
figures. Just one time you wrote a phrase, in black chalk:
It hurts me too. It didn't last two hours, and that time the
police themselves made it disappear. Afterward you went on
only making sketches.

When the other one appeared next to yours you were
almost afraid, suddenly the danger had become double, someone like you had been moved to have some fun on the brink
of imprisonment or something worse, and that someone, as if
it were of no small importance, was a woman. You couldn't
prove it yourself, but there was something different and better
than the most obvious proofs: a trace, a predilection for warm
colors, an aura. Probably since you walked alone you were

imagining it out of compensation; you admired her, you were afraid for her, you hoped it was the only time, you almost gave yourself away when she drew a sketch alongside another one of yours, an urge to laugh, to stay right there as if the police were blind or idiots.

A different time began, at once stealthier, more beautiful and more threatening. Shirking your job you would go out at odd moments in hopes of surprising her. For your sketches you chose those streets that you could cover in a single quick passage; you came back at dawn, at dusk, at three o'clock in the morning. It was a time of unbearable contradiction, the deception of finding a new sketch of hers beside one of yours and the street empty, and that of not finding anything and feeling the street even more empty. One night you saw her first sketch all by itself; she'd done it in red and blue chalk on a garage door, taking advantage of the worm-eaten wood and the nail heads. It was more than ever she—the design, the colors—but you also felt that that sketch had meaning as an appeal or question, a way of calling you. You came back at dawn, after the patrols had thinned out in their mute sweep, and on the rest of the door you sketched a quick seascape with sails and breakwaters; if he didn't look at it closely a person might have said it was a play of random lines, but she would know how to look at it. That night you barely escaped a pair of policemen, in your apartment you drank glass after glass of gin and you talked to her, you told her everything that came into your mouth, like a different sketch made with sound, another harbor with sails, you pictured her as dark and silent, you chose lips and breasts for her, you loved her a little.

Almost immediately it occurred to you that she would be looking for an answer, that she would return to her sketch the way you were returning now to yours, and even though the danger had become so much greater since the attacks at the market, you dared go up to the garage, walk around the block, drink endless beers at the café on the corner. It was absurd because she wouldn't stop after seeing your sketch, any one of the many women coming and going might be her. At dawn on the second day you chose a gray wall and sketched a white triangle surrounded by splotches like oak leaves; from the same café on the corner you could see the wall (they'd already cleaned off the garage door and a patrol, furious, kept coming back), at dusk you withdrew a little, but choosing different lookout points, moving from one place to another, making small purchases in the shops so as not to draw too much attention. It was already dark night when you heard the sirens and the spotlights swept your eyes. There was a confused crowding by the wall, you ran, in the face of all good sense, and all that helped you was the good luck to have a car turn the corner and put on its brakes when the driver saw the patrol wagon, its bulk protected you and you saw the struggle, black hair pulled by gloved hands, the kicks and the screams, the cut-off glimpse of blue slacks before they threw her into the wagon and took her away.

Much later (it was horrible trembling like that, it was horrible to think that it had happened because of your sketch on the gray wall) you mingled with other people and managed to see an outline in blue, the traces of that orange color that was like her name or her mouth, her there in that truncated sketch that the police had erased before taking her away, enough remained to understand that she had tried to answer your triangle with another figure, a circle or maybe a spiral, a form full and beautiful, something like a yes or an always or a now.

You knew it quite well, you'd had more than enough time to imagine the details of what was happening at the main barracks; in the city everything like that oozed out little by little, people were aware of the fate of prisoners, and if sometimes they got to see one or another of them again, they would have preferred not seeing them, just as the majority were lost in the silence that no one dared break. You knew it only too well, that night the gin wouldn't help you except to make you bite your hands with impotence, cry, crush the pieces of colored chalk with your feet before submerging yourself in drunkenness.

Yes, but the days passed and you no longer knew how to live in any other way. You began to leave your work again to walk about the streets, to look fleetingly at the walls and the doors where you and she had sketched. Everything clean, everything clear; nothing, not even a flower sketched by the innocence of a schoolboy who steals a piece of chalk in class and can't resist the pleasure of using it. Nor could you resist, and a month later you got up at dawn and went back to the street with the garage. There were no patrols, the walls were perfectly clean; a cat looked at you cautiously from a doorway when you took out your chalk and in the same place, there where she had left her sketch, you filled the boards with a green shout, a red flame of recognition and love, you wrapped your sketch in an oval that was also your mouth and hers and hope. The footsteps at the corner threw you into a felt-footed run, to the refuge of a pile of empty boxes; a staggering drunk approached humming, he tried to kick the cat and fell face down at the foot of the sketch. You went away slowly, safe now, and with the first sun you slept as you hadn't slept for a long time.

That same morning you looked from a distance: they hadn't erased it yet. You went back at noon: almost inconceivably it was still there. The agitation in the suburbs (you'd heard the news reports) had taken the urban patrols away from their routine; at dusk you went back to see that a lot of people had been seeing it all through the day. You waited until three in the morning to go back, the street was empty and dark. From a distance you made out the other sketch, only you could have distinguished it, so small, above and to the left of yours. You went over with a feeling that was thirst and horror at the same time; you saw the orange oval and the violet splotches where a swollen face seemed to leap out, a hanging eye, a mouth smashed with fists. I know, I know, but what else could I have sketched for you? What message would have made any sense now? In some way I had to say farewell to you and at the same time ask you to continue. I had to leave you something before going back to my refuge where there was no mirror anymore, only a hollow to hide in until the end in the most complete darkness, remembering so many things and sometimes, as I had imagined your life, imagining that you were making other sketches, that you were going out at night to make other sketches.

CLONE

CLONE *(klōn)*, n. Biol. *a group of organisms derived from a single individual by various types of asexual reproduction.*

Random House Dictionary
of the English Language

Everything seems to revolve around Gesualdo: whether he had the right to do what he did or whether he took revenge on his wife for something he should have taken revenge on himself for. Between rehearsals, taking a break in the hotel bar, Paola argues with Lucho and Roberto, the others play canasta or go up to their rooms. He was right then, Roberto insists, and today it's the same thing, his wife cheated on him and he killed her, just another tango, Paolita. Your macho nonsense, Paola says, tangos, sure, but there are women writing tangos now and they're not always singing the same tune. You have to look deeper, timid Lucho suggests, it's not so easy to know why people cheat and why they kill. Maybe in Chile, Roberto says, you people are so refined, but those of us who come from La Rioja shove in a shiv and that's that. They laugh, Paola orders a gin and tonic, it's true that you have to look deeper, for what's behind it, Carlo Gesualdo found his wife in bed with another man and killed them or had them killed—that's the police report on the twelve-thirty news—everything else (and certainly the real news is hiding in everything else) would have to be looked into and that's not so easy after four centuries. There's a lot of bibliography on Gesualdo, Lucho reminds them, if you're so interested go check it out when we get back to Rome in March. A good idea, Paola admits, what remains to be seen is whether or not we'll get back to Rome.

Roberto looks at her without speaking, Lucho lowers his head and then calls the waiter to order another round. Are you referring to Sandro? Roberto asks when he sees that Paola's lost again in Gesualdo or in the fly that's buzzing near the ceiling. Not concretely, Paola says, but you can see that things aren't going so easy now. It'll pass, Lucho says, it's nothing but a whim and a tantrum at the same time, Sandro won't go beyond that. Yes, Roberto admits, but in the meantime the group has to pay for the broken china, we're rehearsing badly and not very much and that's going to be noticed in the end. True, Lucho says, we're singing clenched, we're afraid of making a mistake. We already did in Caracas, Paola says. At least the audience doesn't know Gesualdo very well, Mario's slip was taken as another harmonic audacity by them. The worst thing will be if one of these days it happens with a Monteverdi, Roberto mutters, him they know by heart, damn it.

It continued to be extraordinary that the only stable couple in the group was Franca and Mario. Looking from a distance at Mario who was talking to Sandro over a score and two beers, Paola said to herself that ephemeral alliances, pairing for a brief good time, hadn't been too common in the group: some weekend for Karen and Lucho (or Karen and Lily, because Karen, you know, and Lily probably out of sheer goodness or to find out what it was like even though Lily and Sandro, the generous breadth of Karen and Lily, in the end). Yes, you had to recognize the fact that the only stable couple and the one that deserved the name was Franca and Mario, with a ring on the finger and all the rest. As for herself, once in Bergamo she'd given in to a hotel room, if that meant anything, all curtains and lace, with Roberto in a bed that looked like a swan, a quick interlude with no tomorrow, as good friends as ever, things like that between two concerts, almost between two madrigals, Karen and Lucho, Karen and Lily, Sandro and Lily. And all such good friends, because, as a matter of fact, real couples were brought together at the end of a tour, in Buenos Aires and Montevideo, waiting there were wives and husbands and children and homes and dogs until the next tour, a sailor's life with the inevitable sailor's parentheses, nothing important, modern people. Until. Because now something had changed ever since. I don't know how to think, thought Paola, loose pieces of things come out of me. We're all too tense, damn it. All of a sudden just like that, looking at Mario and Sandro differently as they argued about music, as if underneath she were imagining a different argument. But no, they weren't talking about that, it was most certain they weren't talking about that. Finally, the fact remained that the only real couple was Mario and Franca even though, of course, it wasn't that that Mario and Sandro were discussing. Although probably underneath, always underneath.

.   .   .

The three of them are going to the beach at Ipanema, at night the group is going to sing in Rio and they have to take advantage. Franca likes to stroll with Lucho, they have the same way of looking at things, as if they only brushed them with the fingers of their eyes, they have such fun. Roberto will tag along at the last minute, a pity, because he sees everything seriously and tries to be an audience, they'll leave him in the shade reading the *Times* and will play ball on the sand, swim, and talk—while Roberto is lost in a half sleep in which Sandro reappears—about Sandro's imperceptible loss of contact with the group, his muffled stubbornness that's making things so bad for everyone. Now Franca will throw the red and white ball, Lucho will leap to catch it, they'll laugh like lunatics with every throw, it's hard to concentrate on the *Times*, it's hard to keep your cohesion when a conductor loses contact the way Sandro has and not through any fault of Franca's, it isn't her fault of course, any more than it's Franca's fault that the ball now falls among the glasses of people drinking beer under an umbrella and she has to run and apologize. Folding the *Times*, Roberto will remember his chat with Paola and Lucho at the bar; if Mario doesn't decide to do something, if he doesn't tell Sandro that Franca will never enter any other game but his, everything will go to hell, Sandro isn't just conducting the rehearsals poorly, he's even singing badly, he's losing the concentration that in its time had also concentrated the group and given it the unity and tonal color that the critics talked so much about. Ball in the water, double chase. Lucho first, Franca diving into a wave. Yes, Mario should have realized (it can't be that he hasn't realized yet), the group is going straight to hell unless Mario decides to settle the matter. But where does the matter begin, where should it be settled, since nothing has happened, since no one can say that anything has happened?

. . .

They're starting to suspect, I know it and what can I do, since it's like an illness, since I can't look at her, give her a cue without that pain and that delight at the same time again, without everything's trembling and sliding like sand, a wind on the stage, a river under my feet. Oh, if somebody else would only lead, if Karen or Roberto would lead so I could blend into the group, a simple tenor among the other voices, maybe then, maybe finally. There the way you see him is how he is now, says Paola, there you have him daydreaming right in the middle of the most fucked-up part of Gesualdo, when you have to measure inch by inch in order not to fuck up, precisely then you're stuck with him as if he were up in the air, God damn it. Child, child, Lucho says, proper women don't say fuck. But what pretext for making the change, talking to Karen or Roberto, without counting on the fact that it isn't certain they'll accept, I've led them for such a long time and it can't be changed just like that, technique apart. Last night was so rough, for a minute I thought one of them was going to tell me during intermission, it's obvious they can't take it anymore. Underneath it all you've got good reason to curse, Lucho says. Underneath it all, yes, but it's idiotic, says Paola, Sandro is more musician than any of us, without him we wouldn't be what we are. What we were, Lucho mutters.

There are nights now when everything seems to stretch out interminably, the old celebration—a little crimped before getting lost in the jubilation of each melody—replaced more and more by a dutiful fulfillment of our trade, trembling while putting on the gloves, Roberto says hoarsely, climbing into the ring and foreseeing that you're going to get clobbered.

Such delicate images, Lucho comments to Paola. He's right, what the fuck, Paola says, for me singing used to be like making love and now it's like jerking off. Look at you, talking about images, Roberto laughs, but it's true, we used to be different people, look, the other day, reading some science fiction, I found the exact word: we were a clone. A what? (Paola). I understand you, Lucho sighs, it's true, it's true, singing and living and even thinking were all one single thing in eight bodies. Like the three musketeers, Paola asks, all for one and one for all? That's it, girl, Roberto concedes, but nowadays they call it clone, which is more chic. And we used to sing and live like a single being, Lucho murmurs, not this dragging off now to rehearsals and concerts, programs that never end, neverever. Endless fear, Paola says, every time I think that somebody is going to goof again, I look at Sandro as if he were a lifeguard and the big idiot is there hanging on Franca's eyes, and to make matters worse every time she can she's looking at Mario. She's doing the right thing, Lucho says, he's the one she should look at. Of course she's doing the right thing but everything's going to hell. So gradually that it's almost worse, a shipwreck in slow motion, Roberto says.

Almost a mania, Gesualdo. Because they loved him, of course, and singing his sometimes almost unsingable madrigals called for an effort that was prolonged in the study of the texts, looking for the best way to link the poems to the melody as the Prince of Venosa had done in his obscure genius way. Each voice, each accent, had to find that elusive center from which the reality of the madrigal was to rise, and not one of the so many mechanical versions that they listened to on records sometimes for comparison had it as they tried to compare, in order to learn, to be a bit Gesualdo, assassin prince, lord of music.

Then the arguments would break out, almost always Roberto and Paola, Lucho more moderate, but hitting the mark, each one in his or her way of feeling Gesualdo, the difficulty of clinging to a different version even though there was a minimal difference from the one desired. Roberto had been right, the clone was breaking up and day by day individuals appeared with their discrepancies, their resistance; finally Sandro, as always, overcame the problem, no one disputed his way of feeling Gesualdo except Karen and sometimes Mario, during rehearsals they were always the ones who suggested changes and found defects, Karen almost poisonously against Sandro (it was an old love that had failed, Paola's theory) and Mario resplendent with musical comparisons, examples, and juridical decisions. As in an ascending modulation the conflicts went on for hours until the compromise or momentary agreement. Every Gesualdo madrigal that they added to the repertory meant a new confrontation, the recurrence, perhaps, of the night the prince had unsheathed his dagger as he looked at the naked, sleeping lovers.

Lily and Roberto listening to Sandro and Lucho who are flexing their intellects after two Scotches. There's talk of Britten and Webern and always, finally, the man from Venosa, today it's an accent that would have to be heavier in "O voi, troppo felici" (Sandro) or letting the melody flow in all of its Gesualdic ambiguity (Lucho). Yes, no, this is how it is, Ping-Pong for the pleasure of the effective shots, barbed answers. You'll see when we rehearse (Sandro), maybe that won't be a good test (Lucho), I'd like to know why, and Lucho, fed up, opening his mouth to say what Roberto and Lily would have said too if Roberto hadn't cut in, mercifully squelching Lucho's words, proposing another drink and Lily yes, the others indeed, with plenty of ice.

But it's getting to be an obsession, a kind of cantus firmus around which the life of the group revolves. Sandro is the first to feel it, formerly that center was the music and around it the lights of eight lives, eight sets, the eight small planets of the Monteverdi sun, the Josquin des Prés sun, the Gesualdo sun. Then Franca gradually ascending in a sound sky, her green eyes intent on the cues, the barely perceptible rhythmic indications, altering without knowing it, dislocating without wanting to, the cohesion of the clone, Roberto and Lily think that in unison while Lucho and Sandro return, calm now, to the problem of "O voi, troppo felici," seek the path with the great intelligence that never fails after the third Scotch of the evening.

Why did he kill her? The usual thing, Roberto tells Lily, he found her in the hideout and in other arms, like Rivero's tango, right then and there the man from Venosa stabbed them in person or maybe his executioners, before fleeing the vengeance of the dead woman's brothers and shutting himself up in castles where over the years the delicate webs of the madrigals could be woven. Roberto and Lily have fun fabricating dramatic and erotic variants because they're fed up with the problem of "O voi, troppo felici" that continues its know-it-all debate on the sofa next to them. You can feel

in the air that Sandro has understood what Lucho was going
to tell him, if the rehearsals go on being what they are now,
everything will get more and more mechanical, will be im-
peccably glued to the score and the text, will be Carlo
Gesualdo without love and without jealousy, Carlo Gesualdo
without dagger or vengeance, in short, an assigned madrigalist
among all the others.

"Let's try it with you," Sandro will propose the next
morning. "It really would be better if you led from now on,
Lucho."

"Don't be an asshole," Roberto will say.

"That's right," Lily will say.

"Yes, let's try with you and see what happens, and if
the others agree, you'll keep on leading."

"No," Lucho, who has blushed and hates himself for
blushing, will say.

"Changing conductors isn't what we need," Roberto will
say. "Really," Lily will say.

"It could be, yes," Sandro will say, "it could be good for
all of us."

"In any case, not me," Lucho will say. "I can't see
myself, what do you expect? I've got my ideas like everybody,
but I know my own incapacities."

"This Chilean is a delight," Roberto will say. "Really,"
Lily will say.

"You people decide," Sandro will say. "I'm going to
bed."

"Inspiration comes while you're sleeping," Roberto will
say. "Really," Lily will say.

.   .   .

He looked for him after the concert, not that things had gone badly, but once more that tightness like a latent threat of danger, of error, Karen and Paola singing without spirit, Lily pale, Franca almost never looking at him, the men concentrating and seeming to be absent at the same time; he himself with voice problems, leading coldly but fearful as the program went along, an enthusiastic Honduran audience that wasn't enough to erase that bad taste in his mouth, that's why he looked for Lucho after the concert and there in the hotel bar with Karen, Mario, Roberto, and Lily, drinking almost without speaking, waiting for bedtime in the midst of listless anecdotes, Karen and Mario went off right away, but Lucho didn't seem to want to break away from Lily and Roberto, he had to stay on unwillingly, with the one for the road stretching out in silence. After all, it would be better if we were what we were the other night again, Sandro said, diving into the water, I was looking for you so I could repeat what I said to you then. Oh, Lucho said, but I'll give you the same answer I gave you then. Roberto and Lily once more to the defense, there are all kinds of possibilities, hey, why insist only on Lucho. Whatever you want, it's all the same to me, Sandro said, drinking down his whiskey in one swig, talk it over among yourselves, let me know what you decide. I vote for Lucho. I'm for Mario, Lucho said. It's not a question of voting now, God damn it (Roberto exasperated and Lily of course not). Okay, we've got time, the next concert is in Buenos Aires in two weeks. I'm going to run up to La Rioja to see the old lady (Roberto, and Lily I've got to buy a handbag). You looked for me to tell me this, Lucho said, that's fine, but something like this has to be explained, everybody here has got his or her theory and you too, naturally, it's time to lay them on the table. In any case, not tonight, Roberto decreed (and Lily of course not, I'm falling asleep on my feet, and Sandro pale, looking at the empty glass without seeing it).

It really fell apart this time, Paola thought after erratic dialogues and consultations with Karen, Roberto, and someone or other else. We won't get beyond the next concert, all the more since it's in Buenos Aires and I know my world. Down there they're going to lay their cards on the table, in the end there's family support and if worse comes to worst I'll go live with Mama and my sister while I wait for another chance.

Everybody's got his or her idea, thought Lucho, who, without talking too much, had been taking soundings on all sides. They'll all arrange things to suit themselves if there's no clone understanding as Roberto would say, but instinct tells me we won't get beyond Buenos Aires without squalls. This time it was too much.

Cherchez la femme. La femme? Roberto knows that it's better to look for the husband when it's a question of finding something solid and certain, Franca as always will be evasive with the movements of a fish wiggling in its fishbowl, great innocent green glances, when all's said and done she doesn't seem to be to blame for anything, so look for Mario and find him. Behind the smoke from his cigar, Mario almost smiling, an old friend has every right, but of course that's it, it started in Brussels six months back, Franca told me right after. What about you? Roberto from La Rioja shove in the shiv. Bah, me, Mario the quiet one, the wise one who enjoys tropical tobacco and great green eyes, I can't do anything old man, if he's involved, he's involved. But her, Roberto wants to say and doesn't.

Paola on the other hand yes, who was going to hobble Paola at the moment of truth. She looked for Mario too (they'd arrived in Buenos Aires the night before, the recital was a week away, the first rehearsal after a rest had been pure routine with no great desire, Jannequin and Gesualdo coming out almost the same, disgusting). Do something, Mario, I don't know what, but do something. The only thing that can be done is not doing anything, Mario said, if Lucho refuses to lead I don't see who's capable of replacing Sandro. You, God damn it. Yes, but no. Then we've got to think you're doing it on purpose, Paola shouted, you're not only letting things slip away right under your nose but on top of that you're leaving us in the lurch. You don't have to raise your voice, Mario said, I can hear you quite well, believe me.

It was just the way I'm telling you now, I shouted at him right in his face and you see how he answers me, the big . . . Shh, girl, Roberto says, cuckold is a dirty word, if you ever use it where I come from you'll have a fight on your hands. I didn't mean to say it, Paola has regrets, nobody knows whether or not they're going to bed together and, after all, what difference does it make if they do go to bed or look at each other as if they were in bed together right in the middle of the concert, that isn't the question. That isn't fair, Roberto says, the one who's looking, the one who's falling apart inside, the one who's acting like a moth around a lamp, the idiot who is tainted is Sandro, no one can reproach Franca, she gave him back that kind of leech he puts on her every time he has

her in front of him. But Mario, Paola insists, how can he
stand it? I suppose he trusts her, Roberto says, and he
certainly is in love with her with no need for leeches or
languid faces. Maybe so, Paola accepts, but why does he
refuse to lead us when Sandro is the first one to agree, when
Lucho himself has asked him and we've all asked him?

Because if vengeance is an art, its forms will of necessity
seek the circumvolutions that render it more subtly beautiful.
It's curious, Mario thinks, that someone capable of conceiving
the universe of sound that rises up from his madrigals should
avenge himself so crudely, so much in the manner of the
cheap thug, when it had been given him to spin the perfect
web, watch his prey fall into it, bleed them gradually,
madrigalize a torture of weeks or months. He looks at Paola,
who is working on and repeating a passage from "Poichè
l'avida sete," smiles at her in a friendly way. He knows very
well why Paola has returned to Gesualdo, why almost all of
them look at him when the talk is about Gesualdo and lower
their eyes and change the subject. "Sete," he tells her, don't
stress "sete" so much, Paolita, you feel the thirst more
strongly if you say the word softly. Don't forget the period,
that way of saying so many things in a quiet way, and even
doing them that way.

They saw them coming out of the hotel together, Mario
was holding Franca by the arm, Lucho and Roberto from the
bar could follow them as they went off slowly, arm in arm,
Franca's hand going around Mario's waist as he turned his
head a little to talk to her. They got into a cab, the downtown
traffic sucked them up into its slow serpent.

"I don't get it, old man," Roberto said to Lucho, "I swear, I don't get it at all."

"You're telling me, bub."

"It's never been clearer than this morning, everything leaped into sight, because it's a question of sight, Sandro's useless fakery as he remembers to fake it too late, the damned fool, and she, just the opposite, singing for him and only for him for the first time."

"Karen put me onto it, you're right, she was looking at him this time, she was the one who was burning him with her eyes, and what those eyes can do when they want to!"

"So there you see," Roberto said, "on one side the worst breakdown we've had since we started, and six hours before the concert, and what a concert, they don't let you get away with it here, you know, on the one hand it's the very evidence that the thing has been done, it's something you feel with your blood or your prostate, I've always been aware of that."

"Almost the exact words of Karen and Paola except for the part about the prostate," Lucho said. "I must be less sexy than you people, but it's transparent for me too this time."

"And on the other side you've got Mario, so happy to go out shopping or have a drink with her, the perfect married couple."

"He must know by now."

"And he lets her give that cheap whore come-on."

"Come off it, Roberto."

"Shit, Chile boy, at least let me let it all hang out."

"You're doing fine," Lucho said, "just what we need before the concert."

"The concert," Roberto said. "I wonder if."

They looked at each other, as was customary they shrugged their shoulders and took out their cigarettes.

No one probably sees them but just the same they must
feel uncomfortable crossing the lobby, Lily will look at Sandro
as if she wanted to tell him something and will hesitate, she'll
stop beside a display window and Sandro, with a vague wave,
will turn toward the cigarette stand and ask for a pack of
Camels, will feel Lily's look on the back of his neck, will pay
and start walking toward the elevators while Lily will break
away from the show window and pass by him as in other
times, as in another fleeting encounter that's revived now and
hurts. Sandro will murmur a "hi," will lower his eyes while
he opens the pack of cigarettes. From the elevator door he'll
see her stop at the entrance to the bar, turn toward him. He'll
carefully light the cigarette and go up to get dressed for the
concert, Lily will go to the bar and ask for a cognac, which
isn't good at that time any more than smoking two Camels in
a row is good when there are fifteen madrigals waiting.

As always in Buenos Aires the friends are there and not
just in the audience but looking for them in the dressing
rooms and backstage, meetings and greetings and pats on the
back, home at last, brother, but look how pretty you are
Paolita, let me introduce you to my fiancé's mother, hey
Roberto you're getting too fat, well hello Sandro, I've been
reading the Mexican critics, great, the sound of a full house,
Mario greeting an old friend who asks for Franca, she must
be around here somewhere, the audience beginning to get
restless, ten minutes to go, Sandro making a calm sign for
them to come together, Lucho getting away from two Chilean
women with autograph albums, Lily almost running, they're

so adorable but you can't talk to all of them, Lucho beside
Roberto taking a quick look and suddenly talking to Roberto,
in less than a second Karen and Paola at the same time
where's Franca, the group is onstage but where in the world
is Franca, Roberto to Mario and Mario how should I know,
I left her downtown at seven o'clock, Paola where's Franca,
and Lily and Karen, Sandro looking at Mario, I told you so,
she was coming back on her own, she'd make it in time, five
minutes, Sandro going over to Mario with Roberto crossing
over quietly, you must know what's going on and Mario I
told you I didn't, pale, looking into the air, a stagehand
talking to Sandro and Lucho, running backstage, she's not
there, sir, they haven't seen her come in, Paola covering her
face and doubling over as if she were going to vomit, Karen
grabbing her and Lucho please, Paola, control yourself, two
minutes, Roberto looking at Mario, silent and pale as silent
and pale perhaps as Carlo Gesualdo leaving the bedroom,
five of his madrigals on the program, impatient clapping and
the curtain still down, she's not there, sir, we've looked
everywhere, she hasn't arrived at the theater, Roberto crossing
over between Sandro and Mario, you did it, where's Franca,
shouting, the murmur of surprise from the other side, the
manager trembling, going to the curtain, ladies and gentlemen,
we ask your indulgence for a moment, Paola's hysterical
shriek, Lucho struggling to hold her back and Karen turning,
going off step by step, Sandro falling apart in the arms of
Roberto who holds him like a dummy, looking at Mario, pale
and motionless, Roberto understanding that it had to be there,
there in Buenos Aires, there Mario, there'll be no concert,
there'll never be another concert, they're singing their last
madrigal for nothingness, without Franca they're singing it
for an audience that can't hear them, that, disconcerted, is
beginning to leave.

NOTE ON THE THEME OF A KING AND
THE VENGEANCE OF A PRINCE

When the moment arrives it's natural for me to write as if someone were dictating to me; that's why I impose strict rules on myself from time to time as a variant of something that might end up being monotonous. In this tale the "catch" consisted in adjusting a still nonexistent narrative to the mold of *A Musical Offering* by Johann Sebastian Bach.

It is well known that the theme of this series of variations in the form of a canon and fugue was given to Bach by Frederick the Great, and that after improvising in his presence a fugue based on that theme—unpleasant and thorny—the master wrote *A Musical Offering*, where the initial theme is reprised in a more diverse and complex way. Bach didn't indicate the instruments to be used with the exception of the trio sonata for flute, violin, and clavichord; ever since even the order of the parts has depended on the will of the musicians performing the work. In this case I have made use of the arrangement for eight instruments contemporary to Bach by Millicent Silver, which allows one to follow the elaboration of each passage in all its details and was recorded by the London Harpsichord Ensemble on Saga XID 5237.

Once I had chosen this version (or after she had chosen it, for it was listening to her that I got the idea of a tale that would follow its course) I let time pass; nothing can be hurried in writing, and apparent forgetfulness, distraction, dreams, and chance all imperceptibly weave their future carpet. I made a trip to the beach carrying a photocopy of the jacket of the record where Frederick Youens analyzes the elements of *A Musical Offering*; I vaguely imagined a tale that immediately seemed too intellectual to me. The rules of the game were threatening: eight instruments had to be trans-

figured into eight characters, eight musical sketches, respond-
ing, alternating, or opposing one another, had to find their
correlation in the feelings, behavior, and relationships of eight
people. Conceiving a literary double of the London Harpsichord Ensemble seemed foolish to me in the degree that a
violinist or flautist does not in his private life cleave to the
musical themes he performs; but, at the same time, the notion
of a body, a group, had to exist in some way from the
beginning, since the short scope of a story wouldn't permit
the effective integration of eight people who had no relation-
ship or contact previous to the narration. A casual conversation brought back to me the recollection of Carlo Gesualdo,
a genius for madrigals and the murderer of his wife; everything fell into place immediately, and the eight instruments
were seen as the component parts of a vocal group; from the
first sentence on, that was how the cohesion of a group could
exist, all of them would know and love or hate each other
since before; and furthermore, naturally, they would sing
Gesualdo's madrigals, noblesse oblige. Conceiving a dramatic
action in that context wasn't hard; attaching it to the successive
movements of *A Musical Offering* held the challenge, I mean
the pleasure the writer proposed before anything else.

That was the necessary literary stew, then; the web in
the depths would have to be shown at its moment, as almost
always happens. To begin, the instrumental distribution by
Millicent Silver found its equivalent in eight singers whose
vocal register kept an analogous relation to the instruments.
This gave:

Flute: Sandro, tenor
Violin: Lucho, tenor
Oboe: Franca, soprano

English horn: Karen, mezzo-soprano
Viola: Paola, contralto
Cello: Roberto, baritone
Bassoon: Mario, bass
Clavichord: Lily, soprano

I saw the characters as Latin Americans, with their home
base in Buenos Aires, where they would offer the last recital
of a long tour that had taken them to different countries. I
saw them at the start of a crisis that was still vague (more for
me than for them), where the only thing clear was the fissure
that was beginning to work on the very cohesion of a group
of madrigalists. I had written the first passages feeling my
way along—I haven't changed them, I don't think I've ever
changed the uncertain beginning of a lot of stories of mine
because I feel it would be the worst kind of betrayal of my
writing—when I came to understand that it was impossible to
adjust the tale to *A Musical Offering* without knowing in
detail what instruments—that is, what characters—would
figure in each passage until the end. Then, with a touch of
wonderment that luckily is still with me when I write, I saw
that the final fragment would have to include all of the
characters *minus one*. And that one, from the first pages
already written, had been the still-uncertain cause of the
fissure that was growing in the group, in what another char-
acter would describe as a clone. In the same moment Franca's
necessary absence and the story of Carlo Gesualdo, which had
underlain the whole process of imagination, were the fly and
the spider in the web. Now I could go ahead, everything had
been consummated since before.

. . .

About the writing itself: Each fragment corresponds to the order which is given in the version of *A Musical Offering* done by Millicent Silver; on one side the development of each passage tries to resemble the musical form (canon, trio sonata, canonical fugue, etc.) and contains exclusively the characters who replace the instruments according to the table above. Therefore it will be useful (useful for curious people, but all curious people tend to be useful) to indicate here the sequence as Frederick Youens lays it out, with the instruments chosen by Mrs. Silver:

Ricercar in three voices: Violin, viola, and cello
Perpetual canon: Flute, viola, and bassoon
Canon in unison: Violin, oboe, and cello
Canon in contrary movement: Flute, violin, and viola
Canon in increasing and contrary movement: Violin, viola, and cello
Canon in ascending modulation: Flute, English horn, bassoon, violin, viola, and cello
Trio sonata: Flute, violin, and continuo (cello and clavichord)
    1. Largo
    2. Allegro
    3. Andante
    4. Allegro
Perpetual canon: Flute, violin, and continuo
"Crab" canon: Violin and viola
"Enigma" canon:
    a. Bassoon and cello
    b. Viola and bassoon
    c. Viola and cello
    d. Viola and bassoon
Canon in four voices: Violin, oboe, cello, and bassoon
Canonical fugue: Flute and clavichord
Ricercar in six voices: Flute, English horn, bassoon,

violin, viola, and cello, with continuo of clavichord
(In the final fragment announced as "for six
voices," the clavichord continuo adds the seventh
performer.)

Since this note is already as long as the story, I have no
scruples about making it a little longer still. My ignorance in
matters of vocal groups is complete, and professionals in the
genre will find ample reasons for merriment here. In fact,
almost everything I know about music and musicians comes
to me from record jackets, which I read with great care and
benefit. This also goes for the references to Gesualdo, whose
madrigals have been with me for a long time. That he killed
his wife is certain; the rest, other possible agreements with
my text, would have to be asked of Mario.

RETURN TRIP
TANGO

*Le hasard meurtrier se dresse au coin
de la première rue.
Au retour l'heure-couteau attend.*

Marcel Bélanger, *Nu et noir*

One goes along recounting things ever so slowly, imagining them at first on the basis of Flora or a door opening or a boy who cries out, then that baroque necessity of the intelligence that leads it to fill every hollow until its perfect web has been spun and it can go on to something new. But how can we not say that perhaps, at some time or another, the mental web adjusts itself, thread by thread, to that of life, even though we might be saying so purely out of fear, because if we didn't believe in it a little, we couldn't keep on doing it in the face of outside webs. Flora, then, and she told me everything little by little when we got together, no longer worked at Miss Matilde's (she still called her that even though she didn't have any reason now to continue giving her that title of respect from a maid of all work). I enjoyed having her reminisce about her past as a country girl from La Rioja who'd come down to the capital with great frightened eyes and little breasts that in the end would be worth more in life for her than any feather duster or good manners. I like to write for myself, I've got notebooks and notebooks, poetry, and even a novel, but what I like to do is write, and when I finish it's like a fellow's slipping aside after the pleasure, sleep comes, and the next day there are other things rapping on your window, that's what writing is, opening the shutters and letting them in, one notebook after another: I work in a hospital, I'm not interested in people reading what I write, Flora or anybody else; I like it when I finish a notebook, because it's as if I'd already published it, but I haven't thought about publishing it, something raps on the window and we're off again on a new notebook the way you would call an ambulance. That's why Flora told me so many things about her life without imagining that later on I would go over them slowly, between dreams, and would put some into a notebook. Emilio and Matilde went into the notebook because it couldn't remain just Flora's tears and scraps of memory. She never spoke to me about Emilio and Matilde without crying at the end. After that I didn't ask her about it for a few days, even steered her to other memories, and one beautiful morning I led her gently back to that story again, and Flora rushed into it again as if she'd already forgotten everything she'd told me, began all over, and I let her because more than once her memory brought back things she hadn't mentioned before, little bits that fitted into other little bits, and, for my part, I was watching the stitches of the suture appear little by little, the coming together of so many scattered or presumed things, puzzles during insomnia or maté time. The day came when it would have been impossible for me to distinguish between what Flora was telling me and what she and I myself had been putting together, because both of us, each in his or her own way, needed, like everybody, to have that business finished, for the last hole finally to receive the piece, the color, the end of a line coming from a leg or a word or a staircase.

Since I'm very conventional, I prefer to grab things from the beginning, and, besides, when I write I see what I'm writing, I really see it, I'm seeing Emilio Díaz on the morning he arrived at Ezeiza airport from Mexico and went down to a hotel on the Calle Cangallo, spent two or three days wandering about among districts and cafés and friends from other days, avoiding certain encounters but not hiding too much either, because at that moment he had nothing to reproach himself for. He was probably slowly studying the terrain in Villa del Parque, walking along Melincué and General Artigas, looking for a cheap hotel or boardinghouse, settling in unhurriedly, drinking maté in his room, and going out to a bistro or the movies at night. There was nothing of the ghost about him, but he didn't speak much and not to many people, he walked on crepe soles and wore a black Windbreaker and brown pants, his eyes quick for the get-up-and-go, something that the landlady of the boardinghouse would have called sneakiness; he wasn't a ghost but he looked like one from the distance, solitude surrounded him like another silence, like the white bandana around his neck, the smoke of his butt, never too far away from those almost too thin lips.

Matilde saw him for the first time—for this second first time—from the window of the bedroom on the second floor. Flora was out shopping and had taken Carlitos along so he wouldn't whimper with boredom at siesta time, it was the thick heat of January and Matilde was looking for some air by the window, painting her nails the way Germán liked them, although Germán was traveling in Catamarca and had taken the car and Matilde was bored without the car to go downtown or to Belgrano, she was already used to Germán's absence, but she missed the car when he took it. He'd promised her another one all for herself when the firms merged, she didn't understand those business matters, but evidently they still hadn't merged, at night she would go to the movies with Perla, would hire a rental car, they'd dine downtown, afterward the garage would pass the bill for the car on to Germán, Carlitos had a rash on his legs and she'd have to take him to the pediatrician, just the idea made him even hotter, Carlitos throwing a tantrum, taking advantage of his father's absence to give her a hard time, incredible how that kid blackmailed her when Germán was away, only Flora, with affection and ice cream, Perla and she would have ice cream too after the movies. She saw him beside a tree, the streets were empty at that time, under the double shadow of the foliage that came together up above; the figure stood out beside a tree trunk, a wisp of smoke rising up along his face. Matilde drew back, bumping into an easy chair, muffling a shriek with her hands that smelled of pink nail polish, taking refuge against the back wall of the room.

Milo, she thought, if that was thinking, that instantaneous vomiting of time and images. It's Milo. When she was able to look out from another window no one was on the corner across the way anymore, two children were coming along in the distance playing with a black dog. He saw me, Matilde thought. If it was he, he'd seen her, he was there in order to see her, he was there and not on any other corner, leaning on any other tree. Of course he'd seen her, because if he was there it was because he knew where the house was. And the fact that he'd gone away the instant he was recognized, seeing her draw back, cover her mouth, was even worse, the corner was filled with an emptiness where doubt was of no use at all, where everything was certainty and threat, the tree all alone, the wind in its leaves.

She saw him again at sundown, Carlitos was playing with his electric train and Flora was humming *bagualas* on the ground floor, the house, inhabited once more, seemed to be protecting her, helping her doubt, tell herself that Milo was taller and more robust, that maybe the siesta-time drowsiness, the blinding light . . . Every so often she would leave the television set and from as far away as possible look out a window, never the same one but always on the upper floor because at street level she would have been more afraid. When she saw him again he was in almost the same place but on the other side of the tree trunk. Night was coming on and his silhouette stood out against the other people passing by, talking and laughing; Villa del Parque coming out of its lethargy and going to cafés and movies, the neighborhood night slowly beginning. It was he, there was no denying it, that unchanged body, the gesture of the hand lifting the cigarette to his mouth, the edges of the white bandana, it was Milo, whom she'd killed five years before after escaping from Mexico, Milo, whom she'd killed with papers put together with bribes and accomplices in a studio in Lomas de Zamora where she had a childhood friend left who would do anything for money and maybe for friendship too, Milo, whom she'd killed with a heart attack in Mexico for Germán, because Germán wasn't a man to accept anything else, Germán and his career, his colleagues and his club and his parents, Germán to get married and set up a family, the chalet and Carlitos and Flora and the car and the country place in Manzanares, Germán and so much money, security, then deciding, almost without thinking about it, sick of misery and waiting, after the second meeting with Germán at the Recanatis', the trip to Lomas de Zamora to entrust herself to the one who had said no at first, that it was an outrage, that it couldn't be done, that it would take a lot of pesos, that all right, that in two weeks, that agreed, Emilio Díaz dead in Mexico of a heart attack, almost the truth because she and Milo had lived like dead people during those last months in Coyoacán, until the plane that brought her back to what was hers in Buenos Aires, to everything that had belonged to Milo before going to Mexico together and falling apart together in a war of silences and deceptions and stupid reconciliations that weren't worth anything, the curtain ready for the new act, for a new night of long knives.

The cigarette was still burning slowly in Milo's mouth as he leaned against the tree, looking unhurriedly at the windows of the house. How could he have found out? Matilde thought, still clinging to that absurdity of thinking something was there, but outside or ahead of any thought. Of course he'd ended up finding out about it, discovering in Buenos Aires that he was dead because in Buenos Aires he was dead in Mexico, finding out had probably humiliated him and lashed him down to the first gust of rage that whipped his face, pulling him into a return flight, guiding him through a maze of foreseeable inquiries, maybe Cholo or Marina, maybe the Recanatis' mother, the old hangouts, the cafés where the gang gathered, the hunches, and thereabouts the definite news, that she'd married Germán Morales, man, but just tell me how can that be, I tell you she got married in church and everything, the Moraleses, you know, textiles and dough, respectability, old man, respectability, but just tell me how can that be since she said, but we thought that you, it can't be, brother. Of course it couldn't be and that's why it was all the more so, it was Matilde behind the curtain spying on him, time immobilized in a present that contained everything, Mexico and Buenos Aires and the heat of siesta time and the cigarette that kept going up to his mouth, at some moment nothingness again, the empty corner, Flora calling her because Carlitos wouldn't take his bath, the telephone with Perla, restless, not tonight Perla, it must be my stomach, you go by yourself or with Negra, it's quite painful, I'd better go to bed, I'll call you tomorrow, and all the time no, it can't be like that, how come they haven't told Germán by now if they knew, he didn't find the house through them, it couldn't have been through them, the Recanatis' mother would have called Germán immediately just for the scene it would cause, to be the first to tell him because she'd never accepted her as Germán's wife, think of the horror, bigamy, I always said she wasn't to be trusted, but nobody had called Germán or maybe they had but at the office and Germán was now far away on a trip, the Recanatis' mother is certainly waiting for him to tell him in person, so she won't lose anything, she or somebody else, Milo had found where Germán lived from somebody, he couldn't have found the chalet by chance, he couldn't be there smoking against the tree by chance. And if he wasn't there now it didn't matter, and double-locking the doors didn't matter, although Flora was a little surprised, the only thing for sure was the bottle of sleeping pills, so that after hours and hours she'd stop thinking and lose herself in a drowsiness broken by dreams where Milo never . . . but in the morning now the shriek when she felt a hand, Carlitos, who wanted to surprise her, the sobbing of Carlitos, offended, and Flora taking him out for a walk, lock the door, Flora. Getting up and seeing him again, there, looking directly at the window without the slightest gesture, drawing back and spying later from the kitchen and nothing, beginning to realize that she was locked up in the house and that it couldn't go on like that, that sooner or later she'd have to go out to take Carlitos to the pediatrician or get together with Perla who was phoning every day and getting impatient and didn't understand. In the orange and asphyxiating afternoon, Milo leaning against the tree, the black Windbreaker in all that heat, the smoke rising up and floating away. Or just the tree, but Milo all the same, Milo all the same, being erased only a little by the pills and the television until the last program.

On the third day Perla arrived unannounced, tea and scones and Carlitos, Flora taking advantage of a moment alone to tell Perla that it couldn't go on like that, Miss Matilde needs distraction, she spends her days locked up, I don't understand, Miss Perla, I'm telling you even if it's not my place to, and Perla smiling at her in the study, you did the right thing, child, I know that you love Matilde and Carlitos very much, I think it's Germán's being away that's depressing her, and Flora without a word lowering her head, the mistress needs distraction, I'm only telling you even if it's not my place to. Tea and the usual gossip, nothing about Perla that made her suspect, but then how had Milo been able, impossible to imagine that the Recanatis' mother would have been silent so long if she knew, not even for the pleasure of waiting for Germán and telling him for the sake of the Lord Jesus or something like that, she tricked you so you'd lead her down the aisle, that's exactly what that old witch would say and Germán falling down out of the clouds, it can't be, it can't be. But, yes, it could be, except that now she didn't even have the confirmation that she hadn't been dreaming, that all she had to do was go to the window, but not with Perla there, another cup of tea, tomorrow we'll go to the movies, I promise, come pick me up in your car, I don't know what's got into me these days, come in your car and we'll go to the movies, the window there beside the easy chair, but not with Perla there, waiting for Perla to leave and then Milo on the corner, peaceful against the wall as if waiting for a bus, the black Windbreaker and the bandana around his neck and then nothing until Milo again.

On the fifth day she saw him follow Flora, who was going to the store, and everything became future, something like the pages remaining in that novel left face down on a sofa, something already written and which it wasn't even necessary to read because it had already happened before being read, had already happened before happening in the reading. She saw them coming back chatting, Flora timid and somewhat mistrustful, saying good-bye on the corner and crossing rapidly. Perla came in her car to pick her up, Milo wasn't there and he wasn't there when they got back late at night either, but in the morning she saw him waiting for Flora, who was going to the market, now he went directly over to her and Flora shook hands with him, they laughed and he took the basket and afterward carried it back filled with the fruit and vegetables, accompanied her to the door, Matilde no longer saw them because the balcony jutted out over the sidewalk, but Flora was taking a long time to come in, they were standing there a while chatting by the door. The next day Flora took Carlitos shopping with her and she saw the three of them laughing and Milo stroked Carlitos on the head, on his return Carlitos was carrying a plush lion and said that Flora's boyfriend had given it to him. So you have a boyfriend, Flora, the two of them alone in the living room. I don't know, ma'am, he's so nice, we met all of a sudden, he went shopping with me, he's so good with Carlitos, you don't really mind, do you, ma'am? Telling her no, that was her business, but she should be careful, a young girl like her, and Flora lowering her eyes and of course, ma'am, he just goes with me and we talk, he owns a restaurant in Almagro, his name is Simón. And Carlitos with a magazine in colors, Simón bought it for me, Mama, that's Flora's boyfriend.

German telephoned from Salta announcing that he'd be back in about ten days, love, everything fine. The dictionary said: bigamy, marriage contracted after widowhood by the surviving spouse. It said: status of a man married to two women or of a woman married to two men. It said: interpretative bigamy, according to canon law, that acquired by a marriage contracted with a woman who has lost her virginity through having prostituted herself or through having declared her first marriage null and void. It said: bigamist, one who marries for a second time without the death of the first spouse. She'd opened the dictionary without knowing why, as if that could change anything, she knew it was impossible to change anything, impossible to go out onto the street and talk to Milo, impossible to appear at the window and summon him with a gesture, impossible to tell Flora that Simón wasn't Simón, impossible to take the plush lion and the magazine away from Carlitos, impossible to confide in Perla, just being there, seeing him, knowing that the novel thrown onto the sofa was written down to the words The End, that she couldn't change anything, whether she read it or not, even if she burned it or hid it in the back of German's library. Ten days and then yes, but what, German returning to office and friends, the Recanatis' mother or Cholo, any one of Milo's friends who'd given him the address of the house, I've got to talk to you Germán, it's something very serious, old man, things would be happening one after the other, first Flora with her cheeks flushed, would you mind, ma'am, if Simón came to have coffee in the kitchen with me, just for a little while? Of course she wouldn't mind, how could she mind since it was broad daylight and just for a little while, Flora had every right to receive him in the kitchen and give him a cup of coffee, and Carlitos had every right to come down and play with Simón, who'd brought him a wind-up duck that walked and everything. Staying upstairs until she heard the knock on the door, Carlitos coming up with the duck and Simón told me he's for the River team, that's too bad, Mama, I'm for San Lorenzo, look what he gave me, look how it walks, but look, Mama, it looks like a real duck, Simón gave it to me, he's Flora's boyfriend, why didn't you come down to meet him?

Now she could look out the windows without the slow useless precautions, Milo no longer standing by the tree, every afternoon he would come at five and spend half an hour in the kitchen with Flora and almost always with Carlitos, sometimes Carlitos would come up before he left and Matilde knew why, knew that in those few minutes when they were alone what had to happen was being prepared, what was already there as in the novel open on the sofa was being prepared in the kitchen, in the house of somebody who could be anybody at all, the Recanatis' mother or Cholo, a week had passed and Germán telephoned from Córdoba to confirm his return, announcing almond paste for Carlitos and a surprise for Matilde, he would stay home and rest up for five days, they would go out, go to restaurants, go horseback riding at the Manzanares place. That night she telephoned Perla just to hear her talk, hanging on to her voice for an hour until she couldn't anymore because Perla was beginning to realize that all that was artificial, that something was going on with Matilde, you should go see Graciela's analyst, you're acting strange, Matilde, believe me. When she hung up she couldn't even go to the window, she knew that it was already useless that night, that she wouldn't see Milo on the corner which was dark now. She went down to be with Carlitos while Flora served him his dinner, she listened to him complain about the soup even though Flora looked at her, expecting her to intervene, to help her before she put him to bed, while Carlitos resisted and insisted on staying up in the living room playing with the duck and watching television. The whole ground floor was like a different zone; she'd never understood too well why Germán had insisted on putting Carlitos's bedroom next door to the living room, so far from them upstairs, but Germán couldn't stand any noise in the morning, so Flora could get Carlitos ready for school and Carlitos could shout and sing, she kissed him by the bedroom door and went back to the kitchen, although she no longer had anything to do there, looked at the door to Flora's room, went over and touched the knob, opened it a little and saw Flora's bed, the bureau with photographs of rock bands and the singer Mercedes Sosa, she thought she heard Flora coming out of Carlitos's bedroom and she closed it quietly and started to look in the refrigerator. I made mushrooms the way you like them, Miss Matilde, I'll bring up your dinner in half an hour since you're not going out; I've also got a pumpkin dessert that turned out very good, just like in my village, Miss Matilde.

The stairway was poorly lighted but the steps were few and wide, she went up almost without looking, the bedroom

door ajar with a beam of light breaking on the waxed landing.
She'd been eating at the little table beside the window for
several days now, the dining room downstairs was so solemn
without Germán, everything fit on a tray and Flora, agile,
almost enjoying the fact that Miss Matilde was eating upstairs
now that the master was away, stayed with her and they talked
for a while and Matilde would have liked Flora to have eaten
with her, but Carlitos would have told Germán and Germán
the discourse on distance and respect, Flora herself would
have been afraid because Carlitos always ended up finding
out everything and would have told Germán. And now what
could she talk about to Flora when the only thing possible
was to get the bottle she'd hidden behind the books and drink
half a glass of whiskey in one swig, choke and pant and pour
herself another drink, almost beside the window opening onto
the night, onto the nothingness there outside where nothing
was going to happen, not even the repetition of the shadow
beside the tree, the glow of the cigarette going up and down
like an indecipherable signal, perfectly clear.

She threw the mushrooms out the window while Flora
prepared the tray with the dessert, she heard her coming up
with that rhythm like a sleigh or a runaway colt that Flora had
when she came up the stairs, told her that the mushrooms were
delicious, praised the color of the pumpkin dessert, asked
for a double cup of strong coffee, and for her to bring her
up another pack of cigarettes from the living room. It's hot
tonight, Miss Matilde, we'll have to leave the windows open
wide, I'll spray some insecticide before we go to bed, I've
already put Carlitos in, he went right to sleep and you saw
how he was complaining, he misses his daddy, poor thing, and
then Simón was telling him stories this afternoon. Tell me if

you need anything, Miss Matilde, I'd like to go to bed early if you don't mind. Of course she didn't mind even though Flora had never said anything like that before, she would finish her work and shut herself up in her room to listen to the radio or knit, she looked at her for a moment and Flora smiled at her, content, she was carrying the tray with the coffee and she went down to get the insecticide, I'd best leave it here on the dresser, Miss Matilde, you can spray it yourself before you go to bed, because no matter what they say, it does have a bad smell, it's best when you're getting ready to go to bed. She closed the door, the colt tripped lightly down the stairs, one last sound of dishes; the night began in exactly that second when Matilde went into the library to get the bottle and bring it over beside the easy chair.

The low light from the lamp barely reached the bed at the back of the room, vaguely visible were one of the night tables and the sofa where the novel had been left, but it wasn't there anymore, after so many days Flora must have decided to put it on the empty shelf in the library. With the second whiskey Matilde heard ten o'clock strike in some distant belfry, she thought that she'd never heard that bell before, counted each ring and looked at the telephone, maybe Perla, but no, not Perla at that hour, she always got annoyed or she wasn't in. Or Alcira, calling Alcira and telling her, just telling her that she was afraid, that it was stupid but maybe if Mario hadn't gone out with the car, something like that. She didn't hear the street door open but it didn't matter, it was absolutely clear that the main door was being opened or was going to be opened and nothing could be done, she couldn't go out to the landing, lighting it with the lamp from the bedroom and looking down into the living room, she couldn't ring the bell for Flora to come, the insecticide was there, the water too for medicine and thirst, the turned-down bed waiting. She went to the window and saw the empty corner; maybe if she'd looked out before she would have seen Milo approaching, crossing the street, and disappearing under the balcony, but it would have been even worse, what could she have shouted to Milo, how could she have stopped him since he was going to come into the house, since Flora was going to open the door and receive him in her room, Flora even worse than Milo at that moment, Flora who would have learned everything, who would have her revenge on Milo by having revenge on her, dragging her down into the mud, on Germán, involving her in a scandal. There wasn't the slightest possibility for anything left, but neither could it have been she who'd cried out the truth, completely impossible was an absurd hope that Milo was only coming for Flora, that some incredible turn of fate had shown him Flora completely separate from the other business, that the corner there had been just any corner for Milo back in Buenos Aires, that Milo didn't know it was Germán's house, didn't know he was dead back there in Mexico, that Milo wasn't looking for her through Flora's body. Staggering drunkenly over to the bed, she pulled off the clothing that clung to her body; naked, she rolled onto her side on the bed and looked for the bottle of pills, the final pink or green port within reach of her hand. It was hard to get the pills out and Matilde piled them up on the night table without looking at them, her eyes lost on the shelves where the novel was, she could see it very clearly, open and face down on the one empty shelf where Flora had put it, she saw the Malayan knife that Cholo had given Germán, the crystal ball on the base of red velvet. She was sure that the door had opened downstairs, that Milo had come into the house, into

Flora's room, was probably talking to Flora or had already begun to undress her, because for Flora that had to be the only reason Milo was there, gaining access to her room in order to undress her and undress himself, kissing her, let me, let me stroke you like this, and Flora resisting and not today, Simón, I'm afraid, let me, but Simón in no hurry, little by little he'd laid her crosswise on the bed and was kissing her hair, looking for her breasts under her blouse, resting a leg on her thighs and taking off her shoes as if playing, talking into her ear and kissing her closer and closer to her mouth, I want you, my love, let me undress you, let me see you, you're so beautiful, moving away the lamp and enwrapping her in shadows and caresses, Flora giving in with a first whimper, the fear that something will be heard upstairs, that Miss Matilde or Carlitos, but no, speak low, leave me like this now, the clothes falling just anywhere, the tongues finding each other, the moans, Simón, please don't hurt me, it's the first time, Simón, I know, stay just like that, be quiet now, don't cry out, love, don't cry out.

She cried out but into Simón's mouth as he knew the moment, holding her tongue between his teeth and sinking his fingers into her hair, she cried out and then she wept under Simón's hands as he covered her face, caressing it, she went limp with a final Mama, Mama, a whimper that passed into a panting and a sweet and soft sob, a my love, love, the bland season of blended bodies, of the hot breath of night. Much later, after two cigarettes against a backrest of pillows, towels between guilt-ridden thighs, the words, the plans that Flora babbled out as in a dream, the hope that Simón was listening, smiling at her, kissing her breasts, moving a slow spider of fingers across her stomach, letting himself go, drowsing, doze off a bit, I'm going to the bathroom and

I'll be right back, I don't need any light, I'm like a night cat,
I know where it is, and Flora no, they might hear you, Simón
don't be silly, I told you I'm like a cat and I know where the
door is, doze off a bit, I'll be right back, that's it, nice and
quiet.

He closed the door as if to add a bit more silence to the
house, naked, he crossed the kitchen and the dining room,
faced the stairs and put his foot on the first step, feeling
around for it. Good wood, a good house Germán Morales has.
On the third step he saw the mark of the beam of light from
under the bedroom door; he went up the other four steps and
put his hand on the knob, opened the door with one push.
The blow against the dresser reached Carlitos in his restless
sleep, he sat up in bed and cried out, he cried out a lot at
night and Flora would get up to calm him, give him some
water before Germán could get angry. She knew she had to
quiet Carlitos because Simón hadn't come back yet, she had
to calm him down before Miss Matilde got worried, she
wrapped herself in the sheet and ran to Carlitos's room,
found him sitting at the foot of the bed staring into space,
shouting with fear, she picked him up in her arms, talking
to him, telling him no, no, she was there, she'd bring him
some chocolate, she'd leave the light on, she heard the in-
comprehensible cry and went into the living room with
Carlitos in her arms, the stairway was illumined by the light
from above, she reached the foot of the stairs and saw them
in the doorway, staggering, the naked bodies wrapped in a
single mass that fell slowly onto the landing, that slipped
down the steps, that without breaking apart rolled downstairs
in a confused tangle until it stopped motionless on the living
room rug, the knife planted in Simón's chest as he spread out
on his back, and Matilde—but that only the autopsy would
show afterward—that she had taken enough sleeping pills

to kill her two hours later, when I arrived with the ambulance and was giving Flora an injection to bring her out of her hysteria, giving Carlitos a sedative, and asking the nurse to stay until relatives or friends got there.

III

PRESS CLIPPINGS

*Although I don't think it's really necessary
to say so, the first clipping is real and the
second one imaginary.*

The sculptor lives on the Rue Riquet, which doesn't seem
like a good idea to me, but in Paris you haven't got much
choice if you're an Argentine and a sculptor, generally two
difficult ways of living in this city. We really don't know each
other too well, through snippets of time that stretch back
twenty years; when he called me to talk about a book with
prints of his most recent work and asked me to do a text to
accompany it, I said what it's always best to say in such cases,
that he should show me some of his sculptures and then we'd
see, or, rather, we'd see then.

I went to his apartment at night and first there was coffee
and some friendly sparring, both of us feeling what is in-
evitably felt when someone shows his work to another person

and that fearful moment comes when bonfires will be lighted or a person has to admit, covering it with words, that the wood was wet and gave off more smoke than heat. And before that, on the telephone, he'd told me about his work, a series of small pieces whose theme was the violence in all the political and geographical latitudes that man inhabits as a man/wolf. We knew something about that, two Argentines, letting the nausea of memories rise up once more, the daily accumulation of fright through cables, letters, sudden silences. While we were talking he was clearing a table; he sat me down in a chair that was just right and began to bring out the pieces, putting them under a carefully placed light, and letting me look at them slowly, and then he turned them gradually; we said practically nothing now, because they had the word and that word was still ours. One after another, until there were ten or so of them, small and filiform, clayish or plaster, born out of wires or bottles patiently wrapped by the work of fingers and spatula, growing out of empty cans and objects underneath that only the sculptor's skill showed me as bodies and heads, arms and hands. It was late at night, all that reached us from the street was the rumble of heavy trucks, the siren of an ambulance.

I was glad that there wasn't anything systematic or too explicative in the sculptor's work, that each piece had something of an enigma about it and that sometimes one had to look for a long time in order to understand the modality that violence assumed there; at the same time, the sculptures seemed to me to be at the same time naive and subtle, in any case without any sense of dread or sentimental exaggeration. Even torture, that last form in which violence takes the place of the horror of immobility and isolation, had not been shown with the doubtful trifle of so many posters and texts and movies that returned to my memory, also doubtful, also ready to hold the images and give them back for who knows what kind of obscure pleasure. I said to myself that if I wrote the text the sculptor had asked me to, if I write the text you ask me to, I told him, it will be a text like these pieces, I'll never let myself be carried along by the facility that all too often abounds in this field.

"That's up to you, Noemí," he said to me. "I know it's not easy, we carry so much blood in our memories that sometimes you feel guilty when you put a limit on it, channel it so it doesn't flood us out completely."

"You're talking to the right person. Look at this clipping, I know the woman who signed it, and I learned other things from what friends told me. It happened three years ago, just as it could have happened last night and can be happening at this very moment in Buenos Aires or Montevideo. Just before leaving to come here I opened a letter from a friend and he'd sent me the clipping. Let me have another cup of coffee while you read it, you really don't have to read it after what you've shown me, but, I don't know, I'd feel better if you read it too."

What he read was this:

The undersigned, Laura Beatriz Bonaparte Bruschtein, domiciled at No. 26 Atoyac, District 10, Colonia Cuauhtémoc, Mexico 5, D. F., wishes to pass the following testimony on to public opinion:

1. Aída Leonora Bruschtein Bonaparte, born May 21, 1951, in Buenos Aires, Argentina, profession, teacher in literacy program.

Fact: At ten o'clock in the morning of December 24, 1975, she was kidnapped by personnel of the Argentine army (601st Battalion) at her place of employment in the Monte Chingolo slum, near the federal capital.

The previous day that place had been the scene of a battle that had left a toll of one hundred dead, including inhabitants of the area. My daughter, after being kidnapped, was taken to the military headquarters of the 601st Battalion.

There she was brutally tortured, the same as other women. Those who survived were shot that same Christmas night. Among them was my daughter.

The burial of those killed in the fighting and of the civilians kidnapped, as was the case of my daughter, was delayed for about five days. All the bodies, including hers, were transferred in mechanical shovels from the battalion to the Lanús police station, from there to the Avellaneda cemetery, where they were buried in a common grave.

I kept on looking at the last sculpture that had remained on the table, I refused to cast my eyes on the sculptor who was reading in silence. For the first time I heard the ticking of a clock on the wall, it was coming from the vestibule and was the only thing audible at that moment in which the street was becoming more and more deserted; the soft sound reached me like a nighttime metronome, an attempt to keep time alive inside that hole where the two of us were stuck in a way, the duration that took in a flat in Paris and a miserable slum in Buenos Aires, that abolished calendars and left us face to face with that, what we could only call that, all epithets exhausted, all expressions of horror fatigued and filthy.

" 'Those who survived were shot that same Christmas night,' " the sculptor read aloud. "They probably gave them sweet rolls and cider, remember that in Auschwitz they passed out candy to the children before sending them into the gas chambers."

He must have seen something in my face, he made a

gesture of apology, and I lowered my eyes and looked for another cigarette.

I received official notice of my daughter's murder in Court No. 8 in the city of La Plata, January 8, 1976. Then I was conducted to the Lanús police station, where, after three hours of interrogation, they told me where the grave was located. All they would show me of my daughter were the hands cut off her body and placed in a jar that carried the number 24. What remained of her body could not be turned over because it was a military secret. The following day I went to the Avellaneda cemetery, looking for stake number 28. The inspector had told me that there I would find "what remained of her because one couldn't call what had been turned over to them bodies." The grave was a patch of recently turned ground, twenty feet by twenty, more or less at the rear of the cemetery. I knew how to locate the grave. It was terrible when I realized how more than a hundred people had been murdered and buried, among them my daughter.

2. In view of this infamous situation and one of such indescribable cruelty, in January 1976 I, domiciled on 730 Calle Lavalle, fifth floor, district nine, in the federal capital, bring charges of murder against the Argentine army. I do it in the same tribunal of La Plata, number 8, civil court.

"You can see, all this is worth nothing," the sculptor said, sweeping his arm through the air. "Worth nothing, Noemí, I've spent months making this shit, you write books, that woman denounces atrocities, we attend congresses and round tables to protest, we almost come to believe that things are changing, and then all you need is two minutes of reading to understand the truth again, to——"

"Shh, I'm thinking things like that right now too," I said with a rage at having to say it. "But if I accepted them it would be like sending them a telegram of support, and, besides, you know very well that tomorrow you'll get up and in a while you'll be shaping another sculpture and you'll know that I'm at my typewriter and you'll think that we're many, even though we're so few, and that difference in strength isn't and never will be any reason to be silent. End of sermon. Did you finish reading? Hey, I've got to go."

He shook his head negatively, pointed to the coffeepot.

As a consequence to this legal recourse of mine, the following things happened:

3. In March of 1976, Adrián Saidón, Argentine, twenty-four years old, employed, my daughter's fiancé, was murdered on a street in the city of Buenos Aires by the police, who informed his father.

His body was not returned to his father, Dr. Abraham Saidón, because it was a military secret.

4. Santiago Bruschtein, Argentine, born December 25, 1918, father of my murdered daughter, mentioned previously, doctor of biochemistry by profession, with a laboratory in the city of Morón.

Fact: on June 11, 1976, at 12 noon, a group of military men in civilian clothes came to his apartment at 730 Calle Lavalle, Apt. 9. My husband, attended by a nurse, was in bed, on the verge of death because of a heart attack and with a prognostication of three months to live. The military men questioned him about me and our children, and added that *"like the Jew bastard you are, you're capable of bringing charges of murder against the Argentine army."* Then they made him get out of bed, and, *beating him*, put him into a car, without letting him bring along his medicine.

Eyewitnesses have affirmed that the army and the police used around twenty cars for the arrest. We have not heard anything more about him since. Through unofficial sources, we were informed that he died suddenly at the beginning of his torture session.

"And here I am thousands of miles away arguing with a publisher about what kind of paper the photographs should have, the format, and the jacket."

"Bah, pal, just now I've been writing a story where I talk, no less, about the psy-cho-log-i-cal problems of a girl at the moment of puberty. Don't start up with autotorture, the real kind is quite enough, I think."

"I know, Noemí, I know, God damn it. But it's always the same thing, we always have to recognize that all this happened in another space, another time. We never were and never will be there, where maybe . . ."

(I remembered something I'd read when I was a girl, in Augustin Thierry, perhaps, a story about how a saint, God knows what his name was, had converted Clovis and his nation to Christianity and was describing the scourging and crucifixion of Jesus, and the king rose up on his throne, shaking his spear and shouting: "Oh, if only I could have been there with my Franks!"—the miracle of an impossible wish, the same impotent rage of the sculptor, lost in his reading.)

5. Patricia Villa, Argentine, born in Buenos Aires in 1952, journalist, worked at the Inter-Press Service, and is my daughter-in-law's sister.

Fact: Along with her fiancé, Eduardo Suárez, also a journalist, she was arrested in September 1976, and they were taken as prisoners to the general headquarters of the federal police of Buenos Aires. A week after their seizure, her mother, who had taken legal action in the case, was informed that unfortunately it had been a mistake. Their bodies have not been returned to their families.

6. Irene Mónica Bruschtein Bonaparte de Ginzberg, twenty-two years old, artist by profession, married to Mario Ginzberg, construction foreman, twenty-four years old.

Fact: On March 11, 1977, at six in the morning, a joint force of army and police came to the apartment where they lived, taking the couple away and leaving behind their small children: Victoria, two years, six months old, and Hugo Roberto, one year, six months, abandoned at the door of the building. We immediately asked for a writ of habeas corpus, I at the consulate in Mexico City and Mario's father in the federal capital.

I have inquired about my daughter Irene and Mario, denouncing that horrendous sequence of events to the United Nations, the OAS, Amnesty International, the European Parliament, the Red Cross, etc.

Up to this time, however, I have received no news as to their place of detention. I have a firm hope that they are still alive.

As a mother, unable to return to Argentina because of the situation of family persecution that I have described, and since legal recourses have been annulled, I ask the institutions and people who fight for the defense of human rights to begin the necessary procedures to return my daughter Irene and her husband, Mario, to me and thus safeguard their lives and liberty. Signed, Laura Beatriz Bonaparte Bruschtein (from *El País*, October 1978, reprinted in *Denuncia*, December 1978).

The sculptor gave me back the clipping, we didn't say very much because we were dropping from lack of sleep, I sensed that he was glad I had agreed to go along with him on his book, and only then did I realize that he had been doubtful up to the last because I'm known to be very busy, maybe selfish, in any case, a writer deeply involved in her own pursuits. I asked him if there was a taxi stand nearby and I went out onto the street that was deserted and cold and too broad, to my taste, for Paris. A gust of wind made me turn up my coat collar, I could hear my heels clicking in the silence, marking out a rhythm in which fatigue and obsessions so often insert a melody that keeps coming back, or a line from a poem, but which only let me see her hands cut off her body and put into a bottle that bears the number twenty-four, only let me see her hands cut off her body, I recovered quickly rejecting the recurrent nausea, forcing myself to take a deep breath, to think about tomorrow's work; I never knew why I crossed to the opposite sidewalk, there was no need to since the street opened onto the Place de la Chapelle, where I might be able to get a cab. It made no difference which sidewalk I went along, I crossed because I crossed, because I didn't even have enough strength left to ask myself why I crossed over.

The little girl was sitting on the steps of a porch that was almost lost among the other porches of the tall and narrow houses barely distinguishable from each other in that particularly dark block. That there should be a child on the edge of a step at that hour of the night and in that loneliness didn't surprise me as much as her position, a little whitish splotch with legs tight together and hands covering her face, something that could also have been a dog or some garbage forgotten at the entrance to the house. I looked vaguely around; a truck was pulling away with its weak lights yellow, on the sidewalk opposite a man was walking hunched over, his head sunk in the raised collar of his overcoat and his hands in his pockets. I stopped, took a close look, the child had thin hair, a white skirt, a pink sweater, and when she removed her hands from her face I saw her eyes and her cheeks and not even the half-darkness could hide the tears, the glow that trickled down to her mouth.

"What's wrong? What are you doing there?"

I heard her breathe deeply, swallow tears and mucus, a hiccup or a pout, I saw her face fully lifted toward me, her tiny red nose, the curve of a mouth that was trembling. I repeated the questions, who knows what I said to her, crouching until I felt her very close.

"My mama," the little girl said, speaking between gasps. "My papa is doing things to my mama."

Maybe she was going to say more, but her arms reached out and I felt her cling to me, weeping desperately against my neck; she smelled dirty, of wet underpants. I tried to take her in my arms and get up, but she drew away from me, looking into the darkness of the hallway. She pointed at something, she started forward, and I followed her, barely glimpsing a stone arch and behind the half-darkness the beginning of a garden. Silently she came out into the open air, it wasn't a flower garden but rather a vegetable patch with low wire fences that marked off planted sections, there was enough light to see the skimpy mastic trees, the poles that supported climbing plants, rags to scare off the birds; toward the center you could make out a low hut patched with zinc and tin cans, from whose small window a greenish light came. There was no lighted lamp in any of the windows of the buildings around the plot, the black walls went up five stories until they merged with a low and cloudy sky.

The little girl had gone directly to the narrow passageway between two vegetable patches that led to the door of
the hut; she turned a little to make sure I was following her
and went into the shack. I know that I must have stopped
there and half-turned, telling myself that the girl had had a
bad dream and was going back to bed, every reason that
reason could produce telling me at that moment how absurd
and perhaps risky it was to go into a strange house at that hour
of the night; maybe I was still telling myself these things
when I went through the half-open door and saw the little
girl waiting for me in a vague entrance full of old furniture
and garden tools. A ray of light filtered through under the
door at the back, and the girl pointed to it and almost jumping
over the rest of the entrance began almost imperceptibly
opening the door. Just beside her, face full in the yellowish
ray of the opening that was slowly growing larger, I smelled
burning, I heard a kind of muffled shriek which was repeated
over and over, interrupted then taken up again; my hand
pushed on the door and I took in the foul room—the broken
stools and beer and wine bottles on the table, the glasses, and
the table covering of old newspapers, beyond that the bed
and the naked body gagged with a dirty towel, her hands and
feet tied to the iron bedstead. His back to me, sitting on a
bench, the girl's papa was doing things to her mama; he was
taking his time, slowly lifting his cigarette to his mouth, letting
the smoke out of his nose slowly while the lighted end came
down to rest on one of the mama's breasts, remained there
for the duration of the gagged shrieks under the towel wrapped
around her mouth and face except for the eyes. Before understanding, accepting being part of that, there was time for the
papa to withdraw the cigarette and bring it up to his mouth
again, time to enliven the lighted end and savor the excellent
French tobacco, time for me to see the body burned from the

stomach to the neck, the purple or red splotches that went up from the thighs and the sex to the breasts where now the lighted end rested again with a careful delicacy, seeking an unscarred spot on the skin. The shriek and the shudder of the body on the bed that creaked under the spasm were mixed with things, with acts that I didn't choose and which I will never be able to explain to myself. Between the man with his back to me and myself there was a broken-down stool, I saw it rise up in the air and fall at an angle onto the papa's head; his body and the stool rolled onto the floor almost at the same second. I had to jump back not to fall too. I had put all my strength into the motion of raising the stool and hitting him; that strength immediately abandoned me, leaving me a staggering simpleton. I know that I looked for support without finding it, that I looked vaguely behind and saw the door half-open, the little girl no longer there and the man on the floor a confused splotch, a wrinkled rag. What came afterward I could have seen in a movie or read in a book, I was there as if not being there, but I was there with an agility and an intent that in a very brief time—if it happened in time—led me to find a knife on the table, cut the bonds that held the woman, pull the towel from her face, and see her get up silently, perfectly silent now as if that were necessary and even essential, look at the body on the floor as it began to contract from an unconsciousness that wasn't going to last, look at me wordlessly, go to the body and grab it by the arms while I held its feet. With a double lift we laid it out on the bed, tied it with the same cords, quickly reset and knotted, tied him and gagged him in that silence where something seemed to vibrate and tremble with an ultrasonic sound. What follows I don't know, I see the woman still naked, her hands pulling off pieces of clothing, unbuttoning pants and lowering them into wrinkles at the feet, I see her eyes on mine, a single

pair of wide-open eyes, and four hands pulling and tearing
and undressing, vest and shirt and shorts, now that I have to
remember it and have to write it, my cursed state and my
harsh memory bring me something else indescribably lived
but not seen, a passage from a story by Jack London where
a trapper in the north struggles to win a clean death while
beside him, turned into a bloody thing that still holds a
glimmer of consciousness, his comrade in adventures howls
and twists, tortured by the women of the tribe who horribly
prolong his life in spasms and shrieks, killing him without
killing him, exquisitely refined in each new variant, never
described but there, like us there, never described and doing
what we must, what we had to do. It's useless to wonder now
why I was involved in that, what was my right and my part
in what was going on under my eyes that without doubt saw,
that without doubt remember how London's imagination must
have seen and remembered what his hand was incapable of
writing. I only know that the little girl wasn't with us after
my entry into the room, and that now the mama was doing
things to the papa, but who knows whether only the mama or
whether once more they were gusts of night, pieces of images
coming back out of a newspaper clipping, the hands cut off
her body and put in a bottle that bore the number twenty-four,
through unofficial sources we found out that he died suddenly
at the beginning of the torture session, the towel over her
mouth, the lighted cigarettes, and Victoria, two years and six
months old, and Hugo Roberto, one year and six months,
abandoned at the door of the building. How could I know
how long it lasted, how could I understand that I too, I too
even though I thought I was on the right side, I too, how
could I accept that I too there on the other side from the
cut-off hands and the common graves, I too on the other side
from the girls tortured and shot that same Christmas night,

the rest is turning my back, crossing the garden patch, bumping against a wire fence and scratching my knee, going out
onto the freezing and deserted street and getting to La
Chapelle and almost immediately finding the taxi that took
me to glass after glass of vodka and a sleep from which I
awoke at noon, lying across the bed and fully clothed, with
my knee bleeding and that perhaps providential headache
that straight vodka brings on when it passes from bottleneck
to throat.

I worked all afternoon, it seemed inevitable and frighten-
ing to me that I was capable of concentrating to such a degree;
at dusk I phoned the sculptor, who seemed surprised at my
early reappearance, I told him what had happened to me, I
spat it out in a single flow of words that he respected, although at times I could hear him coughing or trying to get a
question in.

"So you see," I told him, "you see I haven't taken too
much time to give you what I promised."

"I don't understand," the sculptor said. "If you mean
the text about—"

"Yes, that's what I mean. I just read it to you, that's the
text. I'll send it to you as soon as I make a clean copy, I don't
want it around anymore."

After two or three days that had been lived in a haze of
pills and drinks and records, anything that could be a barrier,
I went out to buy some food, the refrigerator was empty and
Cuddles was mewing at the foot of my bed. I found a letter
in the mailbox, the sculptor's thick handwriting on the
envelope. There was a sheet of paper and a newspaper clipping, I began to read while I walked toward the market and
only afterward did I realize that when I had opened the
envelope I had torn and lost a piece of the clipping. The

sculptor was thanking me for the text to his album, unusual
but to all appearances very much like me, far removed from
the usual things in albums, although that didn't bother him
any more than it bothered me. There was a postscript: "A
great dramatic actress has been lost in you, although luckily
an excellent writer has been saved. The other afternoon I
thought you were telling me something that had really happened to you, then by chance I read *France-Soir*, from which
I have taken the liberty of clipping the source of your
remarkable personal experience. It's true that a writer can
argue that if his inspiration comes from reality, and even
from the crime news, what he is capable of doing with it
raises it to another dimension, gives it a different value. In
any case, my dear Noemí, we're too good friends for you to
have felt it necessary to prepare me in advance for your text
and unfold your dramatic talents on the telephone. But let's
leave it at that, you know how much I appreciate your col-
laboration and I'm very glad that . . ."

I looked at the clipping and saw that I had inadvertently
torn it, the envelope and the piece stuck to it were thrown
away somewhere. The news item was worthy of *France-Soir*
and its style: an atrocious drama in a suburb of Marseilles,
the macabre discovery of a sadistic crime, ex-plumber bound
and gagged on a cot, the corpse, et cetera, neighbors furtively
aware of repeated scenes of violence, small daughter missing
for several days, neighbors suspecting abandonment, police
looking for mistress, horrendous spectacle offered to the—the
clipping broke off there, when the sculptor had licked the
envelope too abundantly he had done the same thing as Jack
London, the same as Jack London and as my memory; but
the photograph of the shack was intact and it was the shack
in the vegetable patch, the wire and the zinc sheeting, the high

walls surrounding it with their blind eyes, neighbors furtively aware, neighbors suspecting abandonment, everything there slapping me in the face from the bits of the news item.

I caught a cab and got out on the Rue Riquet, knowing that it was stupid and doing it because that's how stupid things get done. In broad daylight it had nothing that matched my memory and even though I walked along looking at every house and crossed over to the opposite sidewalk as I remembered having done, I couldn't recognize any entranceway that looked like the one from that night, the light fell onto things like an infinite mask, porches but not that porch, no access to an inner garden, simply because that garden was in the suburbs of Marseilles. But the little girl was there, sitting on the steps of some entrance or other, she was playing with a rag doll. When I spoke to her she ran off to the first door, a concièrge came out before I could call to her. She wanted to know if I was a social worker, certain that I had come for the little girl whom she had found lost in the street, that very morning some gentlemen had been there to identify her, a social worker would come to get her. Although I already knew it, before leaving I asked what her last name was, then I went into a café and on the back of the sculptor's letter I wrote the end to the text and went to slip it under his door, it was proper that he should know the ending, so that the text accompanying his sculptures would be complete.

TEXT IN A
NOTEBOOK

The matter of a passenger survey came up—it must be said
—while we were talking about indetermination and analytic
residues. Jorge García Bouza had made some allusions to the
Montreal subway before concretely mentioning the Anglo line
in Buenos Aires. He didn't tell me so, but I suspect he had
had something to do with technical studies by the system—
since it was the system itself that organized the survey. With
special procedures that my ignorance categorizes as such
(although García Bouza insisted on their effective simplicity)
an exact count had been made of passengers using the subway
every day during a certain week. Since he was also interested
in finding out the percentage of inflow at the various stations
on the line, as well as trips from one end to the other or be-

tween intermediate stations, the survey was made with the tightest control possible at all entrances and exits from Primera Junta to Plaza de Mayo. In those days, I'm talking about the forties, the Anglo line still hadn't been connected to the newer underground networks, which made the survey easier.

On Monday of the chosen week a basic total figure was obtained; on Tuesday the figure was approximately the same; on Wednesday, with an analogous total, the unexpected was produced: as against 113,987 people entering, the figure of those who had returned to the surface was 113,983. Common sense called for four errors in calculation, and those responsible for the operation went over the survey positions looking for possible negligence. Chief Inspector Montesano (I'm speaking now from data that García Bouza didn't know about and that I got hold of later) even went so far as to increase the personnel assigned to the survey. Being ever so scrupulous, he had the subway dragged from one end to the other, and workers and train personnel had to show their ID cards as they left. This all makes me see now that Chief Inspector Montesano had vague suspicions at the start of what concerns both of us now. Let me add unnecessarily that no one found the supposed error, which ended up suggesting (and at the same time eliminating) four passengers who were impossible to find.

On Thursday everything went fine; 107,328 inhabitants of Buenos Aires reappeared obediently after their episodic underground immersion. On Friday (after the preceding operations the survey could now be considered perfect), the figure of those who came out again was one greater than that of those tabulated upon entry. On Saturday equal figures were obtained and the system considered the task completed. The anomalous results weren't made public, and except for Chief

Inspector Montesano and the technicians running the adding machines at the Once station, I think few people were aware of what had happened. I also think that those few (I continue to make an exception of the chief inspector) reasonably forgot by the simple attribution of error to the machines or their operators.

This took place in 1946 or early in 1947. During the months that followed I had occasion to use the Anglo line a lot; from time to time, because the trip was long, the memory of that chat with García Bouza would come back to me, and I was ironically puzzled as I looked at the people around me on the seats or hanging from the straps like sides of beef on a hook. Twice, at the José María Moreno station, it seemed to me, unreasonably, that some of the people (a man, later on two old women) weren't ordinary passengers like the others. One Thursday night at the Medrano station, after going to the fights and seeing Jacinto Llanes win on points, it seemed to me that the girl half-asleep on the second bench on the platform wasn't there waiting for the uptown train. She did in fact get on the same car as I did but only to get off at the Río de Janeiro station and stay on the platform as if she were doubtful about something, as if she were terribly tired or bored.

I'm saying all this now that there's nothing left for me to know anymore; in the same way too that after a robbery you remember some suspicious-looking guys walking around the block. And yet, from the beginning, there was something about these fantasies woven in distraction that went farther and left behind a kind of sediment of suspicion; that's why on the night that García Bouza mentioned the results of the survey as a curious detail, the two things became immediately associated and I felt that something was coming together in strangeness, almost in fear. Maybe, of those on the outside, I was the first to know.

This was followed by a confused period where there was a mixture of a growing desire to verify suspicions, a dinner at El Pescadito that brought me close to Montesano and his recollections, and a progressive and cautious descent into the subway understood as something else, as a slow and different breathing, a pulse that in some unthinkable way wasn't beating along with the city, wasn't just another means of transportation in the city anymore. But before I really began descending (I'm not referring to the trivial fact of circulating through the subway like everybody else) there was a time of reflection and analysis. For three months, during which time I preferred taking streetcar number 86 so as to avoid verifications or deceptive coincidences, I was kept up on the surface by a theory of Luis M. Baudizzone that merits attention. Since I had mentioned—almost as a joke—García Bouza's information to him, he thought it was possible to explain the phenomenon by a kind of atomic attrition that is predictable in large multitudes. No one has ever counted the people leaving the River Plate stadium after a championship game on Sunday, no one has compared that figure with those of the box office. Does a herd of five thousand buffalo running through a draw have the same count coming out as going in? The rubbing together of people on the Calle Florida subtly erodes coat sleeves, the backs of gloves. The contact among 113,987 passengers on crowded trains that shake them and rub them against each other at every curve and stop can have, as a result (through the nullification of individuality and the action of erosion on the crowd-creature), the nullification of four units by the end of twenty hours. For the second anomaly, I mean that Friday when there was one passenger extra,

Baudizzone could only agree with Montesano and attribute it to some mistake in arithmetic. At the end of these rather literary conjectures, I felt myself very much alone again—I, who didn't have any conjectures of my own and, in fact, a slow cramp in the stomach every time I came to a subway entrance. That's why on my own I followed a spiral path that was slowly getting closer and closer to the truth. That's why I used the streetcar so much before I felt myself capable of going back to the Anglo line, of really descending, not just going down to take the subway.

It must be said here that I haven't had the slightest bit of help from them, quite the contrary; expecting it or seeking it would have been foolish. They're there and they don't even know that their written history begins with this very paragraph. For my part, I wouldn't like to give them away, and, in any case, I won't mention the few names I got to know during those weeks when I was in their world; if I've done all this, if I'm writing this report, I think my reasons were good, I wanted to help the people of Buenos Aires, always afflicted by transportation problems. Not even that matters now, I'm afraid now, I no longer feel like going down there now, but it's not fair to have to travel slowly and uncomfortably on the streetcar when the subway that everybody else takes because no one is afraid is only two steps away. I'm honest enough to recognize that if they're expelled—without any uproar, without anyone learning too much—I'll feel a lot more comfortable. And not just because my life was obviously in danger while I was down there, but I didn't feel safe either while I went ahead with my investigation that took up so many nights (everything there happens at night, there's nothing falser or more theatrical than the sunlight pouring through the gratings between two stations or rolling down the stairs that lead to the stations); it's quite possible that something has finally given me away and they already know why I spend so many hours in the subway in the same way that I can immediately spot them among the crowds all jammed together in the stations. They're so pale, they proceed with such manifest efficiency; they're so pale and so sad, almost all of them are so sad.

Curiously, what has bothered me most from the start has been finding out how they lived, without any reason for that life to be of the least importance to me. Almost immediately I rejected the idea of sidings or abandoned tunnels; the existence of all of them was manifest and coincided with the coming and going of the passengers between stations. It's true that between Loria and Plaza Once you can catch sight of a vague kind of Hades full of forges, sidings, piles of materials, and strange little huts with blackened windows. That kind of Nibelheim is glimpsed for a few seconds as the train shakes us almost brutally on the curves at the entrance to the station that's so bright in contrast. But it was enough for me to think of all the workers and foremen who share those dirty galleries to dismiss them as a usable redoubt; they wouldn't have exposed themselves there, not during the early days at least. I needed only a few observation trips to realize that nowhere, outside of the line itself—I mean the stations and their platforms and the trains in almost permanent motion—was there a place or conditions that could lend themselves to their life. I went along eliminating sidings, switch-offs, and storerooms until I arrived at the clear and horrible truth through what was of necessity left behind, residual, there in that twilight realm where the idea of being left behind kept returning time and time again. The existence that I am sketching out (some are probably saying that I'm proposing it) appeared to me to be conditioned by the most brutal and implacable necessity; out of the successive rejections of possibilities the only possible solution left was emerging. They, it had become only too clear now, aren't localized anywhere; they live on the subway, on the trains of the subway, moving continually. Their existence and their circulation like leukocytes—they're so pale!—favors the anonymity that has protected them so far.

Having reached this conclusion, I found the rest obvious. Except at dawn and very late at night, the Anglo trains are never empty because Buenos Aires people are night owls and there are always a few passengers coming and going before the station gates are closed. One might imagine now a last useless train that runs along following its schedule even though no one is getting on any longer, but I never got to see that. Or rather, yes, I did get to see it a few times but it was empty really only for me; the few passengers belonged to them, continuing their night through the fulfillment of inflexible instructions. I was never able to locate the nature of their necessary refuge during the three idle hours when the Anglo branch shuts down, from two to five in the morning. Either they stay on a train that's going onto a siding (and in that case the motorman has to be one of them) or they mingle episodically with the nocturnal cleaning people. This last is the least probable, for reasons of dress and personal relationships, and I prefer to suspect the use of the tunnel, unknown to regular passengers, that connects the Once station with the docks. Besides, why is the room with the sign No Admittance at the José María Moreno station full of rolls of toilet paper, not to mention a strange large chest where things can be stored? The visible fragility of that door lends itself to the worst of suspicions; but all in all, even though it might not be too reasonable, my impression is that in some way they continue the existence that has already been described without leaving the trains or the station platforms; an aesthetic necessity underneath it all gives me the certainty, perhaps the reason. There don't seem to be any valid residues in that permanent circulation that carries them back and forth between the two terminals.

I've mentioned aesthetic necessities, but maybe the reasons are only pragmatic. The plan demands a great simplicity so that each one of them can react mechanically and without any mistakes to the successive moments that comprise their permanent life underground. For example, as I was able to verify after much patience, each one knows that he or she mustn't make more than one trip in the same car so as not to draw attention; on the other hand, at the Plaza de Mayo terminal it's all right for them to stay in their seats, since the congestion causes a lot of people to get on the train at Florida in order to get a seat and get the jump on those waiting at the terminal. At Primera Junta the operation is different, all they have to do is get off, walk a few feet, and mingle with the passengers getting on the train across the platform. In every case they have the advantage that the enormous majority of passengers aren't going the whole way. Since they'll only take the subway again much later, within thirty minutes if they're going on a short errand and eight hours if they're office or factory workers, it's unlikely that they'll recognize the ones who stay down there, particularly since they're continually changing cars and trains. This last change, which was hard for me to verify, is much more subtle and is in response to an inflexible pattern destined to prevent possible visual imprints on trainmen or passengers who coincide with them (two times in five, depending on the time and crowding of the public) on the same trains. I know now, for example, that the girl who was waiting at Medrano that night had gotten off the train before mine and had gotten on the one behind us after traveling as far as Río de Janeiro; like all of them, she had precise instructions that went through the end of the week.

Practice has taught them how to sleep in their seats, but only for periods of a quarter of an hour maximum. Even those of us who travel episodically on the Anglo end up having a tactile memory of the itinerary, entry into the few curves on the line infallibly tells us whether we're leaving Congreso in the direction of Sáenz Peña or going up toward Loria. With them the habit is such that they awake at the precise moment to get off and change cars or trains. They sleep with dignity, erect, their heads inclined slightly over their chests. Twenty quarter-hour periods are sufficient to give them rest and, in addition, in their favor they have those three hours forbidden to my knowledge when the Anglo is closed to the public. The day I came to know that they were in possession of at least one train, which confirmed, perhaps, my hypothesis about the siding during closing time, I said to myself that their life must have taken on an almost agreeable community value if it had been given them to travel all together on that train. Quick but delicious collective meals between stations, uninterrupted sleep on a trip from terminal to terminal, even the joy of dialogue and contacts among friends and—why not?—relatives. But I came to ascertain that they strictly abstained from getting together on their train (if it's only one, since their number is doubtless gradually growing); they know only too well that any identification would be fatal for them, and that memory records three faces together at one time, as certain pleonasts say, more easily than mere isolated individuals.

Their train affords them a fleeting clandestine council when they need to receive and hand out the new weekly tabulation that Number One, the first of them, prepares on the pages of a small notebook and distributes every Sunday to the group chiefs; there they also receive money for the week's food, and one of Number One's emissaries (the train's motorman no doubt) listens to what each one has to tell him in matters of clothing, messages to the outside, and state of health. The schedule consists of such an alteration of trains and cars that any meeting is practically impossible and their lives are far apart again until the end of the week. I presume —I've come to understand all this after tense mental projections, imagining myself to be them and suffering or enjoying as they do—that they look forward to each Sunday as we up here look forward to the peace of ours. That Number One had chosen that day is not in response to any traditional respect, which would have surprised me in them; he simply knows that on Sundays there is a different type of passenger on the subway and therefore trains are more anonymous than on a Monday or Friday.

By delicately putting together so many pieces of the mosaic, I was able to understand the initial phase of the operation and the taking of the train. The first four, as the survey figures verify, went down one Tuesday. That afternoon, on the Sáenz Peña platform, they studied the caged faces of the passing motormen. Number One made a sign, and they boarded a train. They had to wait until they left Plaza de Mayo, making use of thirteen stops along the way, and having

the conductor in another car. The hardest part was finding a
moment when they were alone; a chivalrous arrangement by
the Transportation Corporation of the City of Buenos Aires
helped them by reserving the first car for women and children
along with a Buenos Aires mannerism that consists of an
obvious disdain for said car. At Perú two ladies were riding
along talking about the sale at the Casa Lamota (which dresses
Carlota) and a boy was sunk in the inadequate reading of
Rojo y Negro (the magazine, not Stendhal). The conductor
was down toward the middle of the train when Number One
went into the car for ladies and knocked discreetly on the door
to the motorman's cabin. The latter opened it with surprise
but not suspecting anything, and the train was already on its
way up to Piedras. They went through Lima, Sáenz Peña, and
Congreso without incident. At Pasco there was a slight delay
in leaving, but the conductor was at the other end of the train
and not concerned. Forty-eight hours later a motorman in
civilian clothes that were a little large on him mingled with
the people coming out at Medrano and gave Chief Inspector
Montesano the displeasure of having the Friday figure raised
by one unit. Number One was already driving his train, with
the other three furtively practicing in order to replace him
when the time came. I needn't mention that little by little
they did the same with the conductors on the trains they were
taking.

Masters of more than one train, they have at their dis-
posal a mobile territory where they can operate with some
security. I will probably never know why the Anglo motormen
gave in to Number One's extortion or bribery, or how the
latter avoids his possible identification when he comes face
to face with other employees, collects his pay, or fills out
forms. I can only proceed peripherally, uncovering one by

one the immediate mechanisms of the vegetative life, the external conduct. It was hard for me to admit that they fed themselves almost exclusively on the products sold in the kiosks in the stations, until I was persuaded that the most extreme rigor governs this existence without gratifications. They buy chocolate bars and almond paste, coconut and sweet-milk candy, nutritive nougats and caramels. They eat them with the indifferent air of one who is treating himself to a tidbit, but when they're traveling on one of their own trains couples dare buy one of those big crepes covered with milk paste and sprinkles, and they eat it shamefacedly, in little pieces, with the joy of a real meal. They've never been able to solve the problem of ordinary eating in a satisfactory way; how many times must they have been hungry, with the candy becoming repugnant to them and the memory of salt, like the blow of a heavy wave on the mouth, will fill them with horrible delight, and with the salt the taste of the unattainable roast, the soup smelling of parsley and celery! (Around those times a grill had been opened at the Once station and sometimes the smoky smell of sausages and loin sandwiches reached the subway platform. But they couldn't make use of it because it was on the other side of the turnstiles, on the platform of the train to Moreno.)

Another difficult part of their lives is clothing. Pants, skirts, and petticoats wear out. They don't damage jackets and blouses very much, but after a time they have to be changed, for security reasons as well. One morning when I was following one of them, trying to learn more about their customs, I discovered the relations they have with the surface. This is how it is: They get out singly at the indicated station on the indicated day and at the indicated time. Someone comes from the surface with a change of clothing (I ascertained afterward that it was a complete set: clean underwear in every case, and a suit or dress ironed occasionally), and the two get on the same car of the next train. There they can talk, the package is passed, and at the following station they change —that's the most painful part—in the always filthy toilets. One station beyond, the same agent is waiting for them on the platform; they ride together to the next station, and the agent returns to the surface with the package of dirty clothes.

By pure chance and after having convinced myself that I now knew almost all of their possibilities in that terrain, I discovered that along with the periodic exchanges of clothing they have a storeroom where they precariously keep a few articles and objects for cases of emergency, perhaps to cover the prime necessities when new ones arrive, the numbers of whom I can't calculate, but which I imagine to be large. A friend had introduced me on the street to an old man who is struggling along as a *bouquiniste* in the stalls of the Cabildo. I was looking for a back number of *Sur*; to my surprise and leading me perhaps to the inevitable, the book dealer took me down into the Perú station and to the left side of the platform where a well-used passageway begins that doesn't have much of a subway look about it. That's where he had his cache of confused piles of books and magazines. I didn't find *Sur*, but on the other hand there was a small door ajar that opened into another room; I saw the back of someone with that ever-so-white neck they all have; at his feet I managed to glimpse a pile of coats, some handkerchiefs, a red scarf. The book dealer thought he was a retailer or concessionaire like himself; I let him think so and I bought a handsome edition of *Trilce*. But in that matter of clothing some horrible things already had been revealed to me. Since they have more money than they can use and aim to spend it (I imagine it must be the same in minimum security prisons) they satisfy inoffensive whims with a vigor that is touching. At that time I was following a blond boy, I always saw him in the same brown suit; he only changed his tie; two or three times a day he would go into the lavatories to do it. One noon he got off at Lima to buy a necktie at the stand on the platform; he took a long time choosing, unable to decide; it was his great escapade, his Saturday spree. In the pockets of his jacket I could see the bulge of his other ties, and I felt something that wasn't far removed from horror.

The women buy themselves handkerchiefs, knickknacks, key chains, everything there's room for in kiosks and purses. Sometimes they get off at Lima or Perú and stand looking into the show windows on the platform where furniture is on display, they look for a long time at bureaus and beds, they look at the furniture with a humble and contained desire, and when they buy the newspaper or *Maribel* they linger in absorption over the ads for sales, perfumes, figurines, gloves. They're also on the point of forgetting their instructions for indifference and coolness when they see mothers taking their children for an outing get on. Two of them, I saw them only a few days apart, left their seats to ride standing near the children, almost rubbing against them; I wouldn't have been too surprised if they'd stroked their hair or given them candy, things that aren't done on the Buenos Aires subway or probably on any subway.

For a long time I wondered why Number One had chosen precisely one of the survey days to bring the other three down. Knowing his methods, although not him yet, I thought it a mistake to attribute it to arrogance, to the desire to create a stir if the difference between the figures was published. More in accord with his reflective wisdom was to suspect that during those days the attention of the Anglo personnel was centered, directly or indirectly, on the survey operations. The taking of the train, therefore, turned out more feasible; even the return to the surface by the replaced motorman wouldn't bring him any dangerous consequences. Only three months later the chance meeting in the Parque Lezama of the ex-motorman and Chief Inspector Montesano, and the latter's taciturn inferences, managed to bring him and bring me to the truth.

At that time—I'm speaking almost of the present—they had three trains in their possession and I think, without being sure, a position in the control booth at Primera Junta. A suicide shortened my last doubts. That afternoon I'd followed one of the women and saw her go into the telephone booth at the José María Moreno station. The platform was almost deserted and I leaned my face against the side panel, feigning the fatigue of people coming home from work. It was the first time I'd seen one of them in a phone booth, and I hadn't been surprised by the girl's furtive and somewhat frightened manner, her moment of hesitation before looking around and going into the booth. I couldn't hear much, some weeping, the sound of a purse opening, blowing her nose, and then, "But the canary, you're taking care of him, aren't you? Are you giving him birdseed every morning, and the little piece of vanilla?" I was surprised at that banality because the voice wasn't a voice sending a message based on any code, tears were wetting that voice, smothering it. I got on a train before she could discover me and I made the whole circuit, continuing a survey of time schedules and changes of clothing. When we got into José María Moreno again she jumped, after crossing herself (they say); I recognized her by the red shoes and the light-colored purse. There was an enormous crowd, with a lot of people surrounding the motorman and the conductor waiting for the police. I saw that they both belonged to them (they're so pale) and I thought that what had happened would test then and there how solid Number One's plans were, because it's one thing to replace someone in the depths and quite another to bear up under a police interrogation. A week passed without anything new, without the least follow-up of a banal and almost everyday suicide; then I began to be afraid to go down.

I know now that there are still many things I don't know, even the most important, but the fear is stronger than I am. During these days I only manage to get to the entrance at Lima, which is my station, I get that hot smell, that Anglo smell, which comes up to the street; I hear the trains pass. I go into a café and consider myself an imbecile, I ask myself how can I quit when I'm so few steps away from the complete revelation. I know so many things, it might be useful to society to reveal what's going on. I know that over the last few weeks they already have eight trains, and that their number is increasing rapidly. The new ones are still unrecognizable because the fading of the skin is very slow and they're doubtless extreme in their precautions; Number One's plans don't seem to have any error, and the result is that it's impossible for me to calculate their numbers. Only instinct told me, when I still had the courage to go down and follow them, that most of the trains are already full of them, that the regular passengers are finding it more and more difficult to travel all the time; and it doesn't surprise me that the newspapers are asking for new lines, more trains, emergency measures.

. . .

I saw Montesano, I told him a few things and I hoped he would guess others. He seemed to mistrust me, to follow any track on his own or, rather, simply to prefer not understanding something that was beyond his imagination, not to mention that of his superiors. I understood that it was useless to talk to him again, that he might accuse me of complicating his life with fantasies that were probably paranoid, especially when he told me, patting me on the back: "You're tired, you should take a trip."

But the trip I should take is on the Anglo branch. I'm a bit surprised that Montesano hasn't decided to take any measures, at least against Number One and the other three, cutting off at the crown the tree that's sinking its roots deeper and deeper into the asphalt and the earth. There's that penned-in smell, you can hear the brakes on a train, and then the gust of people climbing the stairs with the bovine look of those who've traveled standing up, crammed together in cars that are always full. I should go over, take them aside one by one and explain; then I hear another train coming in and my fear returns. When I recognize one of the agents going down or coming up with the package of clothing, I hide in the café and don't dare go out for a long time. I think, over two glasses of gin, that as soon as I get my courage back I'll go down and check on their numbers. I believe that they've got all the trains now, the administration of many stations, and a part of the repair shops. Yesterday I thought that the saleslady at the candy kiosk at Lima might inform me indirectly about the recent increase in her sales. With an effort that barely overcame the cramps clutching at my stomach, I managed to go down to the platform, repeating to myself that it wasn't a matter of getting on a train, mingling with them; just two questions and going back up to the surface, safe again. I put the coin in the turnstile and went over to the kiosk; I was going to buy a Milkibar when I saw that the saleslady was staring at me. Pretty, but so pale, so pale. I ran desperately toward the stairs, stumbled up. Now I know that I can't go back down; they know me, they've finally gotten to know me.

I've spent an hour in the café without having decided to take the first step onto the stairway again, standing there among the people going up and down, ignoring those who look at me out of the corners of their eyes without understanding that I can't make up my mind to move in a zone where everybody is moving. It seems almost inconceivable to me to have come to the end of the analysis of their general methods and be incapable of taking the final step that will allow me the revelation of their identities and their aims. I refuse to accept the fear that tightens my chest like this. Maybe I'll make up my mind, maybe the best thing would be to hang on to the railing of the stairs and shout out what I know about their plan, what I think I know about Number One (I'll say it even if Montesano is displeased that it's upsetting his own investigation), and, above all, the consequences of all that for the people of Buenos Aires. Up till now I've been writing in the café, the peacefulness of being on the surface and in a neutral place fills me with a calm that I didn't have when I went down to the kiosk. I feel that in some way or other I'm going back down, that I'll make myself, step by step, go down the stairs, but in the meantime the best thing would be to finish my report, send it to the commissioner or chief of police, with a copy to Montesano, and then I'll pay my check and will certainly go down, of that I'm sure, even though I don't know how I'm going to do it, where I'm going to get the strength to go down step by step now that they know who I am, now that they've finally ended up knowing who I am, but that doesn't matter anymore, before I go down I'll have the rough draft ready, I'll say Dear Mr. Commissioner or Dear Mr. Chief of Police, there's someone walking around down there, someone who goes along the platforms and when no one notices, when only I can know and listen, shuts herself up in a dimly lighted booth and opens her purse. Then she weeps, first she weeps a little, and then, Mr. Commissioner, she says, "But the canary, you're taking care of him, aren't you? Are you giving him birdseed every morning, and the little piece of vanilla?"

STORIES I TELL MYSELF

I tell myself stories when I sleep alone, when the bed seems larger than it is and colder, but I also tell them to myself when Niágara is there and falls asleep in the midst of pleasant murmurs, almost as if she too were telling a story. More than once I wanted to wake her up to find out what her story was about (there's been only one murmur so far, and that's not enough for a story), but Niágara always comes back so tired from work that it wouldn't be fair or nice to wake her up when she's just fallen asleep and seems sunken, lost in her perfumed and murmuring little snail shell, so I let her sleep and tell myself stories, the same as on days when she has the night shift and I sleep alone in that suddenly enormous bed.

The stories I tell myself can be anything, but almost always with myself in the main role, a kind of Buenos Aires Walter Mitty who imagines himself in anomalous or silly situations or ones that are intensely dramatic and exaggerated so that the person following the story will enjoy the melodrama or the banality or the humor that the person telling it puts in. Because Walter Mitty also has his Jekyll-and-Hyde side, Anglo-Saxon literature has of course made inroads on his unconscious and the stories are almost always born to him in a bookish way and as if all ready for an equally imaginary press. The very idea of writing down the stories I tell myself before falling asleep seems inconceivable in the morning, and, besides, a man has to have his secret luxuries, his quiet extravagances, things that others would take advantage of down to the last crumb. And there's also superstition. I've always told myself that if I put any of the stories that I tell myself into writing, that story would be my last, for a reason that escapes me but has something to do perhaps with notions of transgression or punishment; no, it's impossible to imagine myself waiting for sleep, alongside Niágara or alone, but unable to tell myself a story, having to count sheep in an imbecilic way or, even worse, to remember my not very memorable daily activities.

Everything depends on the mood of the moment, because it would never occur to me to choose a certain type of story when I or we turn out the light and I enter that second and beautiful cover of darkness that my eyelids bring, the story is there, an almost always stimulating beginning of a story, it might be an empty street with a car coming from way far off, or Marcelo Macía's face when he finds out he's been promoted, something inconceivable until that moment, given his incompetence, or simply a word or sound that's repeated five or six times and out of which the first image of the story begins to emerge. Sometimes I'm surprised that after an episode that could be classified as bureaucratic, the next night the story is erotic or connected to sports; I do have an imagination, no doubt about it, even if it's only evident before I fall asleep, but such an unpredictably varied and rich repertory never ceases to surprise me. Dilia, for example—why did Dilia have to appear in that story and precisely in that story, when Dilia wasn't a woman who lent herself in any way to such a story? Why Dilia?

A long time ago, however, I decided not to ask myself why Dilia or the Trans-Siberian or Muhammad Ali or any of the settings where the stories I tell myself are staged. If I remember Dilia at this moment out of the story now it's for other reasons that were and are also out of it, because of something that isn't the story anymore, and maybe that's why I'm obliged to do what I wouldn't have wanted to do or couldn't have done with the stories I tell myself. In that story (alone in bed; Niágara wouldn't be back from the hospital until eight in the morning) there was a mountain scene and a road that engendered fear, made you drive carefully, the headlights sweeping away the always possible visual traps at every curve, alone and at midnight in that huge truck that was difficult to drive on a road that was like a cornice. Being a truck driver had always seemed to be an enviable occupation to me because I imagine it to be one of the simplest forms of freedom, going from one place to another in a truck, which at the same time is a home with a mattress where you can spend the night on a tree-lined road, a lantern to read by, and cans of food and beer, a transistor to listen to jazz with surrounded by perfect silence, and also that sense of knowing that you're being ignored by the rest of the world, that no one

is aware of the fact that you've taken that route and not another, so many possibilities of towns and adventures on the
trip, including holdups and accidents where I always come
out on top like Walter Mitty.

Sometimes I've wondered why a truck driver and not an
airplane pilot or captain of an ocean liner, knowing at the
same time that it fits my simple and earthy side that I've had
to hide more and more during the day. Being a truck driver
is people who talk to truck drivers, places where a truck driver
moves about, so when I tell myself a story about freedom it
frequently starts in that truck crossing the pampa or going
through an imaginary landscape like the one now, the Andes
or the Rocky Mountains, in any case, on that night a difficult
road I was climbing along when I saw Dilia's fragile figure at
the base of the rocks, violently pulled out of nothingness by
the beam of the headlights, the purple walls making the image
of Dilia even smaller and more forlorn as she gave me the
gesture used by people asking for help, after having walked
so long with a knapsack on her back.

Since being a truck driver is a story I've told myself
many times, it's not hard to find women asking for a lift as
Dilia was doing, although, of course, I'd put them there because those stories almost always capped a fantasy in which
night, truck, and solitude were the perfect accessories for a
brief moment of happiness at the end of the period. Sometimes not, sometimes it was only an avalanche from which I
escaped God knows how, or the brakes that gave out on the
downgrade so that everything ended in a whirlwind of changing visions that made me open my eyes and refuse to go on,
seeking sleep or Niágara's warm waist with the relief of
having escaped the worst. When the story put a woman beside
the road, that woman was always a stranger, the whims of

the stories opting for a redhead or a mulatto girl, seen perhaps in a movie or a magazine picture and forgotten on the surface of the day until the story brought her out without my recognizing her. Seeing Dilia was more than a surprise therefore, almost a scandal, because Dilia had nothing to do with that route and in some way she was ruining the story with her expression—somewhere between imploring and undermining. Dilia and Alfonso are friends that Niágara and I see from time to time, they live in a different orbit and the only things that bring us together are a faithful friendship since university days, common tastes, a dinner from time to time at their place or here; we keep track of them from a distance as a couple with a baby and a bit of money. What in the devil did Dilia have to do here where the story was happening in a way in which any imaginary girl yes but not Dilia, because if there was anything clear in the story it was that this time I would meet a girl on the way and out of it would come some of the many things that can happen when you reach the flats and make a stop after the long tension of the crossing; everything so clear from the first image, dinner with other truck drivers at the lunch room in the town before the mountains, a story no longer original at all but always pleasing because of its variants and unknown women, except that now the unknown woman was different, it was Dilia, who made no sense whatever on that curve in the road.

It might be that if Niágara had been there murmuring and softly snorting in her sleep I would have preferred not bringing Dilia up, erasing her and the truck and the story by just opening my eyes and saying to Niágara, "That's funny, I was on the point of going to bed with a woman and it was Dilia," so that maybe Niágara would open her eyes in turn and kiss me on the cheek, calling me silly or getting Freud

into the act or asking me if I'd ever wanted Dilia sometime,
in order to hear me tell the truth, but never in this rotten life,
although then Freud again or something like that. But feeling
myself so alone in the story, as alone as I was, a truck driver
in the midst of crossing the mountains at midnight, I wasn't
capable of passing by: I slowly braked, opened the door, and
let Dilia get in as she scarcely murmured a "thanks" full of
fatigue and sleep and stretched out on the seat with her pack
by her feet.

The rules of the game are observed from the first moment
in the stories I tell myself. Dilia was Dilia but in the story I
was a truck driver and only that for Dilia, it never would have
occurred to me to ask her what she was doing there in the
middle of the night or call her by her name. I think that in
the story the exceptional thing was that that girl should con-
tain the person of Dilia, her straight blond hair, her blue
eyes, and her legs almost conventionally evoking those of a
colt, too long for her figure; outside of that, the story treated
her like any other girl, without any name or previous connec-
tion, a perfect fateful meeting. We exchanged two or three
phrases, I gave her a cigarette and lighted another, we began
going downhill as a heavily loaded truck should, while Dilia
stretched out even more, smoking with an abandonment and
drowsiness that washed away all her hours of walking and
maybe fear on the mountain.

I thought she was going to fall asleep right away and
that it was pleasant to imagine her like that until reaching the
flats there below us. I thought that maybe it would be a
friendly gesture to invite her to get into the back of the truck
and stretch out on a real bed, but never in a story have things
allowed me to do that, because any of the girls would have
looked at me with that expression that was somewhere between

bitter and desperate out of which she imagines the immediate intentions, almost always looking for the door handle, the necessary flight. In the stories just as in the presumptive reality of any truck driver things couldn't happen that way, you'd have to talk, smoke, make friends, get out of all that the almost always silent acceptance of a stop in the woods or a rest area, the acquiescence for what would come later but which was no longer bitterness or anger, simply sharing what was already being shared since the talk, the cigarettes, and the first beer drunk out of the bottle between two curves.

I let her sleep, then, the story had that development, which I've always liked in the stories I tell myself, the minute description of every thing and every act, a film in very slow motion for a pleasure that goes progressively along, climbing up through body and words and silences. I still wondered why Dilia that night but I immediately stopped wondering, it seemed so natural to me now—Dilia there half-asleep beside me, accepting another cigarette from time to time or murmuring an explanation of why there in the middle of the mountains—that the story got embroiled between yawns and broken phrases since nothing could have explained why Dilia was there in the loneliest spot on that road at midnight. At some moment she stopped talking and looked at me, smiling, that girl's smile that Alfonso described as a shopper's smile, and I gave her my truck driver's name, always Oscar in any of the stories, and she said Dilia and added as she always added that it was an idiotic name, the fault of an aunt who read gooey novels, and almost incredibly I thought that she didn't recognize me, that in the story I was Oscar and that she didn't recognize me.

Afterward came all that the stories tell me but I can't

tell it the way they do, only uncertain fragments, threads that
might be false, the lantern lighting up the folding table in the
back of the truck parked among the trees at a rest stop, the
sputter of fried eggs, then the cheese and sweets, Dilia looking
at me as if she were going to say something and deciding that
she wouldn't say anything, that it wasn't necessary to explain
anything, to get out of the truck and disappear under the
trees, I making things easier with the coffee almost ready and
even a shot of grappa, Dilia's eyes as they would close between drink and phrase, my careless way of moving the lamp
to the little table beside the mattress, adding a blanket in case
later on the cold, telling her I was going up front to lock the
doors just in case, you never knew on those deserted stretches
and she lowering her eyes and saying, you know, don't stay
there and go to sleep on the seat, it would be idiotic, and I
turning my back so she wouldn't see my face where there was
probably a vague surprise at what Dilia was saying although
of course it always happened that way in one form or another,
sometimes the little Indian girl would talk about sleeping on
the ground or the gypsy would take refuge in the cab and I
would have to take her by the waist and lead her inside, carry
her to the bed even though she cried or struggled, but not
Dilia, Dilia slowly moving from the table to the bed with one
hand already searching for the zipper on her jeans, those
movements that I could see in the story even though my back
was turned and I was going into the cab to give her time, to
tell myself yes, that everything would be the way it had to
be one more time, an uninterrupted and perfumed sequence,
the very slow dolly shot of the motionless figure in the headlights at the curve in the mountain to Dilia now almost invisible under the wool blankets, and the cut as always, putting

out the lantern so that all that was left was the vague ember of the night coming in through the rear window with the occasional plaint of a nearby bird.

That time the story lasted interminably because neither Dilia nor I wanted it to end, there are stories that I would like to prolong, but the little Japanese girl or the cold, condescending Norwegian tourist won't let them go on, and in spite of the fact that I'm the one who decides in the story, a moment comes when I haven't got the strength or even the desire to make something last after the pleasure begins to slip into insignificance, there where you would have to invent alternatives or unexpected incidents for the story to stay alive instead of carrying me off to sleep with a last distracted kiss or the remains of an almost useless moan. But Dilia didn't want the story to end. From her first gesture when I slipped in beside her, instead of the expected I felt her searching for me; from the first double caress I knew that the story had only just begun, that the night of the story would be as long as the night in which I was telling the story. Only now there's nothing left but this, words talking about the story; words like matches, moans, cigarettes, laughter, entreaties, and demands, coffee at daybreak and a dream of heavy waters, of night dew and returns and abandonments, and a first timid tongue of sun coming through the window to lick Dilia on the shoulder as she lay stretched out on top of me, blinding me while I held her tightly and felt her open up once more amidst cries and caresses.

The story ends there, without any conventional good-byes in the first town on the way as would have been almost inevitable, from the story I passed into sleep with nothing but the weight of Dilia's body as she fell asleep in turn after one last murmur, when I woke up Niágara was talking to me about breakfast and a date we had for that evening. I know that I was on the point of telling her and something held me back, something that might have been Dilia's hand returning me to the night and forbidding me words that would have soiled everything. Yes, I'd slept quite well; of course, at six o'clock we would meet on the corner of the square and go see the Marinis.

Around that time Alfonso had told us that Dilia's mother was quite ill and that Dilia was going to Necoches to be with her, Alfonso had to take care of the baby, who was giving him a lot of trouble, how about our visiting them when Dilia got back. The sick woman died a few days later and Dilia didn't want to see anybody until two months later; we went to dinner, bringing them some cognac and a rattle for the baby and everything was fine now, Dilia finishing a duck à l'orange and Alfonso with the table set up to play canasta. The dinner rolled along pleasantly as it should have because Alfonso and Dilia are people who know how to live and they began by talking about the most painful thing, quickly exhausting the theme of Dilia's mother, then it was like softly drawing a curtain so as to return to the immediate present, our usual games, the key words and codes of the humor that made it so agreeable to spend the evening with them. It was already late and cognac when Dilia mentioned a trip to San Juan, the need to forget her mother's last days and the problem with those relatives who complicate everything. It seemed to me she was talking to Alfonso, although Alfonso must have known the story already because he was smiling pleasantly while he served us another cognac, the breakdown of the car in the middle of the mountains, the empty night and the interminable wait by the side of the road where every night bird was a menace, the inevitable return of so many childhood ghosts, the lights of a truck, the fear that maybe the driver would also be afraid and pass her by, the blinding from the lights striking the stone walls, then the wonderful squeal of the brakes, the warm cab, the descent with unnecessary dialogues but which did so much to make her feel better.

"She's been traumatized," Alfonso said. "You already told me, sweetheart, each time I learn more details about that rescue, about your Saint George in coveralls saving you from the wicked dragon of the night."

"It's not easy to forget," Dilia said, "it's something that keeps coming back, I don't know why."

Maybe she didn't, maybe Dilia didn't know why but I did, why I had to drink the cognac down in one gulp and pour myself another while Alfonso raised his eyebrows, surprised at a brusqueness he didn't recognize in me. His jokes, on the other hand, were more than predictable, telling Dilia that sometime she should decide to finish the story, he knew the first part only too well, but was sure that it had a second part, there was so much ravine, so much truck in the night, so much everything that's so much in this life.

I went to the bathroom and stayed awhile trying not to look at myself in the mirror, not to find there too and horribly the thing I'd been while I was telling myself the story and which I felt again now but here, now, tonight, the thing that was slowly beginning to take over my body, the thing I had never imagined possible all through so many years of Dilia and Alfonso, our friendly double pairing at parties and movies and kisses on the cheek. Now it was the other thing, it was Dilia afterward, the desire again but on this side, Dilia's voice reaching me from the parlor, laughter from Dilia and Niágara who must have been teasing Alfonso about his stereotyped jealousy. It was late now, we drank still more cognac and had one last coffee, the baby's crying came from upstairs and Dilia ran up, brought him down in her arms, he was all wet the little pig, I'm going to change him in the bathroom, Alfonso enchanted because that gave him another half hour to argue with Niágara about the possibilities of Vilas versus Borg, another cognac, girl, after all, we're all immune now.

Not me, I went to the bathroom to keep Dilia company as she laid her son out on a little table and looked for things in a cupboard. And it was as if she knew in some way when I said to her Dilia, I know that second part, when I told her I now know it can't be but you see, I know it, and Dilia turned her back to me to start undressing the baby and I saw her lean over not only to undo the safety pins and take off the diaper but also as if she were suddenly overwhelmed by a weight that she had to free herself from, from which she was already freeing herself when she turned, looking me in the eyes and said yes, it's true, it's idiotic and it has no importance but it's true, I went to bed with the truck driver, tell Alfonso if you want, in any case he's convinced in his own way, he doesn't believe it but he's so sure.

That's how it was, I wouldn't say anything and she wouldn't understand why she was saying that to me, why to me, who hadn't asked her anything and, on the other hand, had told her what she couldn't understand on this side of the story. I felt my eyes going down across her mouth, her throat like fingers, seeking her breasts under the black blouse, I sketched again how my hands had sketched all that night, all that story. Desire was a crouching leap, an absolute right to look for her breasts under the blouse and enwrap her in the first embrace. I saw her spin, lean over again but now light, freed from the silence; she deftly removed the diaper, the smell of the baby who'd peed and pooed reached me along with Dilia's murmuring, calming him so he wouldn't cry, I saw her hands as they picked up the cotton and put it between the baby's uplifted legs, I saw her hands cleaning the baby instead of coming to me as they had come in the darkness of that truck that has served me so well so many times in the stories I tell myself.

MOEBIUS STRIP

In memoriam J. M. and R. A.

Impossible to explain. She was leaving that
zone where things have a fixed form and
edges, where everything has a solid and
immutable name. She was sinking deeper
and deeper into the liquid, quiet, and
unfathomable region where vague and cool
mists like those of morning hovered.

Clarice Lispector
Close to the Savage Heart

Why not, maybe it would have been enough just to try as
she would try eagerly later on and she would be seen, she
would be felt, with the same clarity that she was seen and
felt pedaling into the woods in the still cool morning, following paths wrapped in the shadow of ferns, in some place in
Dordogne that the newspapers and radio would later fill with
a fleeting infamous celebrity until quick oblivion, the vegetable silence of that perpetual half-light through which Janet
passed like a blond splotch, a tinkle of metal (her canteen
poorly fastened onto the aluminum crossbar), her long hair
offered to the air that her body broke and altered, a light-
weight figurehead sinking her feet into the soft alternation of

the pedals, receiving on her blouse the hand of the breeze grasping her breasts, a double caress with the double defile of tree trunks and ferns in a tunnel-green translucence, a smell of mushrooms and bark and moss, vacation time.

And the other woods too, even if they were the same woods, but not for Robert, turned away at farms, dirty from a night face down on a poor mattress of dry leaves, a ray of sunlight that filtered through the cedars, stroking his face, vaguely wondering if it was worth the trouble to stay in the region or go to the flatlands where maybe a pitcher of milk and a little work was awaiting him before going back to the highways or getting lost in the nameless woods, always the same woods, with hunger and that useless rage that twisted his mouth.

At the narrow crossroads Janet put on the brakes indecisively, right or left or straight ahead, all equally green and cool, held out like the fingers of a great earthen hand. She'd left the youth hostel at daybreak because the dormitory was full of heavy breathing, fragments of others' nightmares, the smell of people scarcely washed, the merry groups that had roasted corn and sung until midnight before lying down on the canvas cots with their clothes on, the girls on one side and the boys farther off, vaguely offended by so many idiotic regulations, half-asleep already despite their useless sarcastic comments. In the open countryside before the woods she'd drunk the milk in the canteen, never again to meet the people of the night before, she too had her idiotic regulations, to cover France while her money and time lasted, to take pictures, to fill her orange-colored notebook, nineteen English years old already with lots of notebooks and pedaled miles, a predilection for open spaces, her eyes dutifully blue and her hair blond, tall and athletic and a kindergarten teacher whose Kinder were happily scattered over beaches and villages in her happily distant homeland. To the left, maybe, there was a slight slope in the shadows, letting herself coast after a simple push on the pedal. It was starting to get hot, the bicycle seat was receiving her heavily, with a first dampness that would later oblige her to get off, unstick her panties from her skin and lift up her arms so that the cool breeze could get under her blouse. It was only ten o'clock, the woods were revealing themselves, slow and deep; perhaps before reaching the road on the opposite side it would be nice to settle down under an oak tree and eat the sandwiches, listen to the pocket radio or add another entry to her travel diary, interrupted so many times by the start of poems and not always happy thoughts that the pencil wrote and then, with embarrassment, with difficulty, scratched out.

> It wasn't easily seen from the path. Without knowing it, he'd slept sixty feet away from an abandoned shed, and now it seemed to him stupid to have slept on the damp ground when behind the pine boards full of holes he saw a floor of dry straw under an almost intact roof. He was no longer sleepy and it was a pity; motionless, he looked at the shed and wasn't surprised that the woman on the bicycle had come along the path and stopped, she was the one who was disconcerted by the structure that rose up among the trees. Before Janet saw him he already knew everything, everything about her and about him in one single wordless wave, taking off from an immobility that was like a future crouching in wait. Now she was turning her head, the bicycle tilted, and one foot on the ground, and she found his eyes. They both blinked at the same time.

There was only one thing that could be done in cases like that, infrequent but always probable: say bonjour and leave without excessive haste. Janet said bonjour and pushed the bicycle to give it a half turn; her foot was lifted from the ground to give the pedal its first push when Robert cut off her way and grabbed the handlebars with a hand that had black nails. Everything was quite clear and confused at the same time, the bicycle tipping over and the first cry of panic and protest, the feet looking for a useless support in the air, the strength of the arms encircling her, the pace—almost a run—through the broken boards of the shed, a smell both young and savage at the same time of leather and sweat, a dark three-day beard, a mouth burning her throat.

> He never wanted to hurt her, he'd never hurt anyone to possess the little that had been given him in the inevitable reformatories, it was only like that, twenty-five years and like that, all at the same time, slow, as when he had to write his name, Robert letter by letter, then the last name even slower, and quick, like the movement that was sometimes worth a bottle of milk or a pair of pants laid out to dry on the grass in a garden, everything could be slow and instantaneous at the same time, a decision followed by a desire for everything to last for a long time, for that girl not to fight absurdly, since he didn't want to hurt her, for her to understand the impossibility of escape or of being rescued and to submit quietly, not even submitting, letting herself go as he was letting himself go, laying her down on the straw and shouting into her ear for her to shut up, not be a fool, to wait while he looked for buttons and fasteners without finding anything but convulsions of resistance, gusts of words in a different

language, shouts, shouts that someone would end up hearing.

It hadn't been exactly like that, there was the horror and the revulsion at the attack by the beast, Janet had struggled to get away and run off and now it was no longer possible and the horror didn't come only from the bearded beast, because he wasn't a beast, his way of speaking into her ear and holding her down without sinking his hands into her flesh, his kisses that fell onto her face and neck with the prickle of the stubble, but kisses, the revulsion came from submitting to that man who wasn't a hairy beast but a man, the revulsion that had always been lying in wait, ever since her first bleeding one afternoon at school, Mrs. Murphy and her warnings to the class in her Cornish accent, the crime news in the paper always commented on secretly at the boarding school, the forbidden books where that wasn't what was hinted at rosily in the books recommended by Mrs. Murphy with or without Mendelssohn and showers of rice, the clandestine comments about the episode of the first night in *Fanny Hill*, the long silence of her best friend back from her honeymoon and then the sudden weeping, clinging to her, it was horrible, Janet, although later with the joy of the first child, the vague evocation of the past one afternoon on a walk together, I was wrong to exaggerate so much, Janet, you'll see one day, but too late now, the idée fixe, so horrible, Janet, another birthday, the bicycle and the plan to travel alone until maybe, maybe little by little, nineteen years old and the second vacation trip to France, Dordogne in August.

Someone would end up hearing her, he shouted into her face although he already knew that she was incapable of understanding, she looked at him rolling her eyes and begging something in another language, fighting to get her legs free, to stand up, for a moment it seemed to him that she was trying to tell him something that wasn't just shouts or pleas or insults in her language, he unbuttoned her blouse blindly looking for the fasteners farther down, holding her onto the straw bedding with his whole body crossed over hers, asking her not to shout anymore, that it wasn't possible for her to go on shouting, somebody was going to come, let me, don't shout anymore, just let me, please, don't shout.

How to stop struggling if he didn't understand, if the words she had tried to tell him in his language came out in pieces, got mixed up with his babbling and his kisses and he couldn't understand that it wasn't a question of that, that horrible as what he was trying to do to her, what he was going to do to her, was, it wasn't that, how to explain to him that up until then never, that *Fanny Hill*, that at least he should wait, that in her bag there was facial cream, that it mustn't be like that, it mustn't be without what she'd seen in the eyes of her friend, the nausea of something unbearable, it was horrible, Janet, it was so horrible. She felt her skirt give way, the hand that ran under her panties and pulled them down, she contracted with a last shriek of anguish and fought to explain, to stop him at the brink so that it would be different, she felt him against her and the attack between her open thighs, a sharp pain that grew until the red and the fire, she howled from horror more than from suffering, as if that couldn't be everything and only the beginning of the torture, she felt his hands on her face covering her mouth and slipping down below, the second attack against the one who could no longer struggle, against which there were no longer shouts or tears.

Plunged in her in a sudden end of struggling, taken in without that desperate resistance that he had had to beat down by impaling her time and time again until he reached the deepest part and felt all her skin against his, the pleasure came like a lash and he dissolved in a thankful babbling, in a blind, interminable embrace. Taking his face out of the hollow of Janet's shoulder, he sought her eyes to tell her so, to thank her for being quiet at last; he couldn't suspect other reasons for that savage resistance, that struggle that had obliged him to rape her without pity, but neither did he understand her surrender, the sudden silence. Janet was looking at him, one of her legs had slowly slipped to the side. Robert began to draw away, come out of her, looking into her eyes. He understood that Janet didn't see him.

Neither tears nor breath, the breath had stopped suddenly, from the depths of her skull a wave had covered her eyes, she no longer had a body, the last thing had been the pain time and again and then halfway through a shriek her breath had suddenly given out, expired without coming in again, replaced by the red veil like blood eyelids, a sticky silence, something that lasted without being, something that was in a different way where everything was still there but in a different way, this side of sense and memory.

She didn't see him, the dilated eyes passed right through his face. Getting free of her he kneeled at her side, talking to her while his hands somehow or other adjusted his pants and he looked for the glittering closing as if working independently, smoothing his shirt and tucking it in. He saw the half-open, twisted mouth, the thread of pink drool slipping down over her chin, the arms crossed with the hands clenched, the fingers motionless and shiny with blood slipping slowly down the half-open thighs. When he shouted, leaping up, he thought for a second that the shout had come from Janet, but from up above, standing like a swaying doll, he saw the marks on her throat, the unacceptable twisting of the neck that turned Janet's head to one side, made something of it that was mocking him with the look of a fallen marionette, all its strings cut.

Different, perhaps from the very beginning, in any case not there, becoming like something diaphanous, a translucent medium in which nothing had a body and where what had been her wasn't located through thoughts or objects, to be wind while being Janet or Janet being wind or water or space but always clear, the silence was light or the opposite or both things, time was illuminated and that was to be Janet, something without a handle, without the slightest shadow of memory to interrupt and fix that course as among crystals, a bubble inside a mass of Plexiglas, the orbit of a transparent fish in a limitless lighted aquarium.

The woodcutter's son found the bicycle on the path and through the boards of the shed he glimpsed the body face up. The police verified that the murderer had not touched Janet's overnight case or purse.

To drift in the immobile with no before or after, a hyaline now without contact or references, a state in which the container and the contained were undifferentiated, water flowing in water, until without transition it was the impetus, a violent rushing projecting her, drawing her along unable to grasp the change in any way except in the dizzy rush on the

horizontal or the vertical of a space that shuddered in its
velocity. Sometimes it would come out of the shapeless and
accede to a rigorous fixedness also separated from all reference and nevertheless tangible, there was that moment when
Janet ceased to be water of water or wind of wind, for the first
time she felt, felt herself closed in and limited, cube of a
cube, motionless cubeness. In that cube state outside the
translucent and the hurricaned, something like a duration was
being installed, not a before or an after but a more tangible
now, a beginning of time reduced to a thick and manifest
present, cube in time. If she had been able to choose she
would have preferred the cube state without knowing why,
perhaps in the continuous changes it was the only condition
where nothing changed as if there she were inside given limits,
in the certainty of a constant cubeness, of a present that hinted
at a presence, almost a tangibility, a present that contained
something that perhaps was time, perhaps an immobile space
where every displacement remained as drawn. But the cube
state could give way to other vertigos and before and after
or during you were in another medium, you were once more
a thunderous sliding through an ocean of crystals or diaphanous rocks, a flowing without direction toward anything, a
tornado suction with whirlwinds, something like sliding along
through the entire foliage of a jungle, held up from leaf to
leaf by a weightlessness of devil's drool and now—now without a before, a dry and given now there—perhaps again the
cube state coming closer and stopping, limits in the now and
the there that in some way were rest.

The trial opened in Poitiers toward the end of July
1956. Robert was defended by Maître Rolland; the
jury would not admit the extenuating circumstances of
early orphanhood, reformatories, and unemployment.

The accused listened to the sentence of death in a peaceful stupor, the applause of an audience among which there were a great number of British tourists.

Little by little (little by little in a condition outside of time? a manner of speaking) other states were presenting themselves, had perhaps already been presented, although *already* would mean before and there was no before; now (or any now either) a wind state prevailed and now a crawling state in which each now was painful, the complete opposite of the wind state because it was only presented as a dragging, a progression to nowhere; if she had been able to think, Janet would have passed to the image of the caterpillar crawling over a leaf suspended in the air, passing over its faces and passing again without the slightest sight or touch or limit, infinite Moebius strip reptation to the edge of a face to arrive at or already to be on the opposite side and to return ceaselessly from one side to the other, a very slow and painful reptation there where there was no measure of slowness or suffering but where one was reptation and being reptation was slowness and suffering. Or the other (the other in a condition without comparable ends?), to be fever, going dizzily through something like pipes or circuits, going through conditions that might be mathematical sets or musical scores, leaping from point to point or note to note, going in and out of computer circuits, being set or score or circuit running through itself and that was given to be fever, given to run furiously through instantaneous constellations of signs or notes without form or sound. In some way it was suffering, the fever. To be the cube state now or be the wave held a difference, it existed without fever or without reptation, the cube state was not fever and being fever was not the cube state or the wave state. In the cube state now—a now suddenly more now—for the first time (a now where an indication of first time had just been given), Janet ceased being the cube state to be in the cube state, and later (because that first differentiation of the now contained the feeling of later) in the wave state Janet ceased being the wave state to be in the wave state. And all that contained the indications of a temporality, now a first time could be recognized and a second time, a being in wave or in fever that succeeded each other to be pursued by a being in wind or being in foliage or being again in cube, being each time more Janet in, being Janet in time, being what was not Janet but which was passing from the cube state to the fever state or returning to the caterpillar state, because more and more the states were becoming fixed and established and in some way delimited not only in time but in space, there was a passing from one to another, passing from a cube placidity to a fever mathematical circuit or foliage equatorial jungle or interminable crystalline bottles or maelstrom whirlpools in hyaline suspension or painful reptation over double-faced surfaces or faceted polyhedrons.

The appeal was denied and Robert was transferred to the Santé to await execution. Only a pardon by the president of the republic could save him from the guillotine. The condemned man spent his days playing dominoes with the guards, smoking endlessly, sleeping heavily. He dreamed all the time, through the peephole of the cell the guards would see him toss on his cot, lift up an arm, shudder.

In some one of the steps the first rudiments of a memory would be born, slipping among the leaves or at the end of the cube state to be in the fever she learned something of what Janet had been, unconnectedly a memory was trying to enter and be fixed, once it was knowing that she was Janet, remembering Janet in a wood, the bicycle, Constance Myers and some chocolates on a nickel-plated tray. Everything was beginning to cluster together in the cube state, was being sketched out and confusedly defined, Janet and the woods, Janet and the bicycle, and with the gusts of images a feeling of person was becoming clearer, little by little, a first disquiet, the vision of a shed of rotten boards, being face up and held down by a convulsive force, fear of pain, the rubbing of a skin that scratched her mouth and face, something abominable was coming close, something was fighting to be explained, to say it wasn't like that, that it shouldn't have had to be that way, and on the edge of the impossible the memory stopped, a spiral running in acceleration until nausea pulled her out of the cube to sink her into wave or into fever, or the opposite, the asphyxiating slowness of crawling once more with nothing else but that, being in reptation, like being in wave or glass was once more only that until another change. And when she fell back into the cube state and returned to a confused recognition, shed and chocolate and quick visions of belfries and fellow students, the little that she could have done fought above all to the last there in the cubeness, to maintain itself in that state where there was detention and limits, where she would end by thinking and recognizing herself. On occasion she reached the last sensations, the scratch of a bearded skin against her mouth, the resistance under hands that were pulling off her clothes before getting lost again instantaneously in a thunderous careening, leaves or clouds or drops or hurricanes or explosive circuits. In the cube state she could not pass from the limit where everything was horror and revulsion but if will had been given her that will would have become fixed there where a sensitive Janet was blooming, where there was Janet wanting to abolish the recurrence. In full struggle against the weight that was crushing her against the straw of the shed, obstinately saying no, that it didn't have to happen that way with shouts and rotten straw, she slipped once more into the moving state in which everything flowed as if being created in the act of flowing, smoke spinning in its own cocoon that opens and wraps around itself, the being in waves, in the indefinable decanting that already so many times had held her in suspension, alga or cork or jellyfish. With the difference that Janet felt coming from something that was like waking up from a dreamless sleep, falling into the awakening one morning in Kent, being Janet and her body again, a notion of body, of arms and back and hair floating in the hyaline medium, in the total transparency because Janet couldn't see her body, it was her body finally again but without her seeing it, it was consciousness of her body floating among waves or smoke, without seeing her body Janet moved, put out an arm and stretched her legs in an impulse of swimming, differentiating herself for the first time from the undulating mass that enwrapped her, swam in water or smoke, was her body and enjoyed with each stroke what was no longer a passive race, an interminable transfer. She swam and swam, she didn't need to see herself swim and receive the grace of a voluntary movement, of a direction that hands and feet imposed on the course. Falling without transition into the cube state was the shed again, remembering again and suffering, once more up to the limit of the unbearable weight, the slashing pain, and the red nausea covering her face, she found herself on the other side, crawling with a slowness that now she could measure and abominate, passed to be fever, to be a rush of hurricane, to be in waves again and enjoying her body Janet, and when at the end of the indeterminate everything coagulated into the cube state, it wasn't horror but desire that was waiting for her on the other side of the end, with images and words in the cube state, with pleasure of her body in the being in waves. Understanding, reunited with herself, invisibly she Janet desired Robert, desired the shed again, desired Robert who had brought her to what she was there and now, understood the madness under the shed and desired Robert, and in the delight of the swimming amidst liquid crystals or strata of clouds on high she called him, stretched out her body face up to him, called him so that he could really consummate in the pleasure the clumsy consummation on the foul-smelling straw of the shed.

It is difficult for the defense attorney to inform his client that the recourse of a pardon has been denied; Maître Rolland vomited when he came out of the cell where Robert, sitting on the edge of his cot, was staring into space.

From pure sensation to recognition, from the fluidity of the waves to the severe cube, coming together into something that was Janet again, desire was looking for its road, another step among the recurrent steps. Will was coming back to Janet, at first memory and sensations had been given without an axis to modulate them, now along with desire will was coming back to Janet, something in her stretched out an arch like one of skin and tendons and viscera, projected her toward what couldn't be, demanded access inside and outside the states that enveloped her and abandoned her dizzily, her will was desire opening a way in liquids and flashing constellations and very slow dragging, Robert was in some way a kind of end, the goal that was being sketched out now and had a name and a touch in the cube state and that after or before in the now agreeable swimming among waves and crystals was resolved in clamor, in a flame caressing her and throwing her to herself. Incapable of seeing herself, she felt herself; incapable of thinking articulately, her desire was desire and Robert, was Robert in some unreachable state but which Janet will sought to force, a Robert state in which the Janet desire, Janet will, wanted to accede as now once more to the cube state, to solidification and delimitation in which rudimentary mental operations were more and more possible, strings of words and memories, taste of chocolate and pressure of feet on chrome pedals, rape in the midst of convulsions of protest where now desire nested, the will of finally giving in amidst tears of pleasure, of thankful acceptance, of Robert.

His calm was so great, his politeness so extreme, that they left him alone at times, came to spy through the peephole or offer him cigarettes or propose a game of dominoes. Lost in his stupor, which in some way had always been with him, Robert didn't feel the passage of time. He let himself be shaved, he went to the shower with his two guards, once he asked about the weather, if it was raining in the Dordogne.

It was being in waves or crystals that a more vehement stroke, a desperate blow with her heel, launched her into a cold and enclosed space, as if the sea had vomited her up into a grotto of shadows and Gitanes smoke. Sitting on the cot, Robert was looking into the air, the cigarette burning between his fingers. Janet wasn't surprised, surprise had no course there, neither presence nor absence; a transparent partition, a cube of diamond inside the cube of the cell, isolated her from every attempt, from Robert there under the electric light. The bow of herself stretched out to the ultimate had no string or arrow against the diamond cube, the transparency was silence of impenetrable material, not a single

time had Robert raised his eyes to look in the direction that
only contained the thick air of the cell, the swirling smoke
from the tobacco. Janet clamor, Janet will, capable of reaching there, of finding, smashed into an essential difference,
Janet desire was a tiger of translucent froth that was changing
shape, stretching out white claws of smoke toward the small
barred window, threading off and getting lost as she twisted
in her inefficacy. Thrown in one last impulse, knowing that
at any moment she could once more be crawling or careening
among a foliage of grains of sand or atomic formulas, Janet
desire demanded the image of Robert, sought to reach his face
or his hair, to call him to her side. She saw him look toward
the door, scrutinize for an instant the peephole empty of
watchful eyes. With an explosive gesture Robert took something out from under the mattress, a vague noose of twisted
blanket. With a leap he reached the window, slipped the noose
through. Janet was howling, calling him, the silence of her
howl smashed against the diamond cube. The investigation
showed that the prisoner had hanged himself by letting himself drop down with all his weight. The jerk must have made
him lose consciousness and he couldn't fight against asphyxia-
tion; scarcely four minutes had passed from the last visual
inspection by the guards. Nothing now, in the full clamor of
the break and the passage to the solidification of the cube
state, broken by the Janet entry into being fever, run up in a
spiral of uncountable alembics, leap to a depth of thick earth
where advance was an obstinate biting of resistant substances,
a sticky climbing up to levels vaguely sea green, a passage
to being in waves, first strokes like a happiness that had a
name now, a propeller reversing its spin, a hopelessness become hope, the steps from one state to another didn't matter
much now, being in foliage or in sonorous counterpoint, now
Janet desire was provoking them, was seeking them with the

bending of a bridge sending itself to the other side of a metal leap. In some condition, passing through some state or all of them at once, Robert. At some moment being fever Janet or being in waves Janet it could be waves Robert or fever or cube state in the now without time, not Robert but cubeness or fever because the nows would let him also pass on to be in fever or in waves, would be giving him Robert little by little, would filter him and drag him along and fix him in a simultaneity sometimes entering the successive, Janet desire struggling against every state to sink itself in the other where still not Robert, to be once more in fever without Robert, to be paralyzed in the cube state without Robert, to enter blandly the liquid where the first strokes were Janet, feeling herself whole and knowing herself Janet, but there some time Robert, there surely some time at the end of the warm swaying in crystal waves a hand would reach Janet's hand, it would at last be Robert's hand.

A NOTE ON THE TYPE

This book was set on the Linotype in Bodoni Book, a type face so called after Giambattista Bodoni, a celebrated printer and type designer of Rome and Parma (1740–1813). Bodoni Book as produced by the Linotype Company is not a copy of any one of Bodoni's fonts, but a composite, modern version of the Bodoni manner. Bodoni's innovations in type style included a greater degree of contrast in the "thick and thin" elements of the letters and a sharper and more angular finish of details.

Composed by Maryland Linotype Company, Inc.,
Baltimore, Maryland
Printed and bound by The Haddon Craftsmen, Inc.,
Scranton, Pennsylvania

Designed by Judith Henry